WRITE TO WOOF
2015

EDITED BY DIANA KATHRYN PLOPA

Grey Wolfe Publishing, LLC
PO Box 1088
Birmingham, Michigan 48009
www.GreyWolfePublishing.com

© 2015 Grey Wolfe Publishing, LLC
Published by Grey Wolfe Publishing, LLC
www.GreyWolfePublishing.com
All Rights Reserved

ISBN: 978-1628280784
Library of Congress Control Number: 2015935171

WRITE TO WOOF 2015

EDITED BY
DIANA KATHRYN PLOPA

DEDICATION

Write To Woof is an annual anthology published by Grey Wolfe Publishing. The goal of this year's collection is to bring awareness to the roles dogs play in our lives... as companions, helpers and teachers. Whether pure-bred or rescued Mutt; each enhances our lives like no other creature on earth.

This book is lovingly dedicated to Darwin. His photo appears on the front cover. He was a tremendous companion and teacher to our family. We miss him dearly.

ACKNOWLEDGEMENTS

We would like to send out a special *Thank You* to the authors who submitted their work for this book. It is because of your dedication to dogs as well as the writing craft that we have been able to produce such a spectacular tribute to our furry friends!

We also want to thank the good people of *Leader Dogs For The Blind* who work tirelessly day after day to make sure that people in need find just the right canine companion to help them see the world in a different light.

And finally, we want to thank *you*, the person who purchased this book and are about to read it. Because of your interest in dogs, or perhaps because of the relationship you have with one of the authors, people with particular challenges will be partnered with extraordinary dogs to help them more quickly achieve the goals and dreams of their lifetime.

CONTENTS

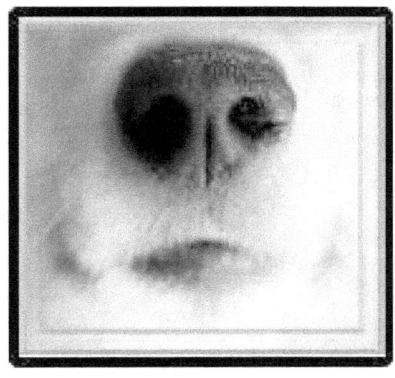

THANK YOU, AUTHORS!

We believe in the power of the pen. We believe that literacy is an essential part of a successful life. We are committed to serving agencies who believe that dogs have a special place in the lives of humans. Again, we asked for your help, and again, you responded with an enthusiasm we could not have anticipated. We are exceedingly grateful!

The goal of this collection is to bring awareness to the exemplary work of the special people at **Leader Dogs For The Blind.** Proceeds from the sales of this book will support their efforts to house, provide veterinary care, and train dogs to serve those who are in need. Their important work is supported primarily through the outreach of the Lion's Clubs of Michigan and through the generous hearts and hands of people like you.

This book is a collection of poetry, short fiction stories and personal essays about dogs. We were thrilled to receive such a diverse collection of words that will most certainly make a difference in the lives of dogs and the people who are their companions!

Remember, your words will always make a difference.
Write To Woof!

1.
A COLD WET NOSE
SHAY CAROLINE SIMMONS

with apologies to Robert Burns

O, my luve he has a coold wet nose,
He came to me in June.
O my luve has his own melodie
That's sweetly howled in tune.

As hoongry art thou, my bonnie lad,
So deep in luve am I,
And I will fill thy bowl, my dear,
Till the kibble bags gang dry.

Till the kibble bags gang dry, my dear,
We'll go walkin' in the soon!
And I will pitch thy toy, my dear,
And after it ye shall roon.

I'm off to work, my oonly luve,
And fare thee weel a while!
I really weel come home, my luve,
Though it were ten thousand mile!

A COLD WET NOSE
SHAY CAROLINE SIMMONS

2.
A PAPER SIGN
SHANNON WAITE

I stared at the sign hanging on the lamppost.

It's mocking me, I thought.

It had to be.

<u>Lost Dog</u>: Help us find our beloved dog, Clover! Reward for finding!

The poorly made poster lay there, tattered, against the grainy wood battered with rusted nails. I looked at it, hopeless because no one had ever made a sign like that for me. As scruffy of a sign as it was, and as tarnished of a place that this piece of printer paper hung, someone still cared... right? And that was what stuck out to me; that was what mattered.

I shook my head, shoved my cold palms further into the pockets of my bright red coat, and I trudged through the rest of the snow that lead down the block to my office job.

"Mary!" was the first thing that I heard being screeched as I walked in. I looked over in Barb's direction.

"The copy machine's down."

I nodded my head, and while taking my coat off, I immediately headed to the back of the office to get right to work; no one around here ever let me waste my time.

Dimly lit room; cramped desks; copy paper chaos; this was my life. I sat on the floor, legs crossed, and I worked my small hands into the awkward crevices of the machine. That's one of the reasons why they liked me: I had small hands. I pulled drawers out, located the jammed paper, and slowly but surely started to clear out the machine.

"Mary," I heard my name again; a word synonymous with disaster. My chest heaved a heavy sigh. Although this time the tone was different, it always meant that something else was wrong.

I turned my head and looked up at Jim, the cute, mid-twenty engineer who was newer to the office - with a year under his belt - compared to the middle-aged men who had been working at the company for decades.

"Jim," I mirrored the statement, turning back to the task at hand.

"I don't ever see you doing anything other than fixing everyone else's problems," he chuckled; a cup of coffee in one hand, he ran his fingers through his hair with his other.

"That's what they pay me for," I muttered.

I squinted my eyes, leaned forward, and worked at a few more buttons and levers until I located one of the other jammed pieces of paper.

"Well, keep it up," he said light heartedly.

I felt a pause – I think he was waiting for me to turn, maybe smile, maybe say something more, but when I didn't, the temperature in the room changed as he walked away.

"You're worth more than that."

I could have sworn that I heard him whisper those words, but I turned and he was gone and already down the hall, high fiving another coworker.

I replayed a slideshow of twenty-five years of my life through my head once I pulled the last jammed paper from the stupid machine sitting in front of me.

Whoever said that technology is a good thing, has never worked in an office. I shut the copy machine's doors, stood up, and flattened the wrinkles in my dress.

"Mary!" came the third call.

I looked up.

My boss was in front of the door, staring at me.

"We're low on printer ink. Janet was supposed to grab some yesterday, but she had some family matters come up, so we're going to need you to run to the store around the block and grab some, please."

I nodded my head. She nodded her's back, turned to leave, mentioned that I should grab my coat because it was cold outside, and then gave a half-hearted smile as she walked back to her desk.

I know that it is cold. I felt it as I walked in. It snowed two inches last night. Thanks for the assistance.

Lifting my coat, I made sure to put both arms in it and pull it on tightly. I put my knitted headband on over my frizzing, black hair, and gloves on my tiny, cold hands.

As I headed directly back to the same place that I had come from a half hour before, I began to pass Jim's desk.

"Mary," he started, "where are you going already?"

"They need printer ink."

He raised an eyebrow.

"It's what they pay me for," I stated.   I had a prewritten response for everything around here.

Jim sighed.

"Mary," he began, "are you okay?"

That was a new end to the very familiar beginning- I did not have a prewritten response for that one.

"Are you flustered?" he snickered when my cheeks flushed rose; a stark contrast to my pale skin and dark locks.

"Well, I - I'm doing... okay."

"Just okay?" he questioned.   He leaned back in his chair so effortlessly.

"Yes." I responded.   After years of commands, I learned that if I hadn't had a practiced response already programmed, that yes was the next best option.

Ending the conversation was then the next step.

"All right, I better get going.   This place runs on everything that gets printed, so I know that I need to go get the ink now."

"Be safe," Jim added as I pushed- not pulled, which is what I mistakenly did the first two months of working there- the door open and welcomed the bitter cold against my body.

I passed that stupid sign again and was faced with the reminder that there were people out there who cared about others; others being other people, other animals, other things, whatever – but people cared.

People cared.

Why didn't I have that?

That slideshow began flipping over again in my mind, as I relived the broken relationships and static heartaches that littered those memories. I re-experienced my mother slapping me when I came in the house too late after I helped our elderly neighbor into her house first. I re-lived the time when my school teacher criticized me for not living up to her expectations when I was caught helping my dyslexic friend with her homework. I remembered the moment that my first boyfriend pushed me out of his car because I didn't give him what he wanted. I don't know what it was that prompted this cinematic experience, but it made me feel heavy.

I took a few deep breaths, hoping that the cold air would freeze the repetitive thoughts. It didn't though, and I cursed everything I was becoming.

This wasn't what I had planned on doing with my life, and these weren't the people I planned on surrounding myself with. After growing up with a mother who treated my name like a curse word, I didn't expect to be working in an environment like that too.

With each step, a new plan started forming. I needed something different... I needed something new.

As I moved forward, I looked at the browns and grays bleeding into the delicate white snow, thanks to the city life with fast feet and faster cars. As I glanced to the right of me, around the corner and ahead to the store that I needed, I noticed a little pup covered in snow from last night's storm. When I realized that no one was down this end of the block, I slowed my pace, hoping that I could get closer to the dog to see if he was the one, missing, posted on the sign a ways back.

"Clover?" I called.

The beagle looked up, peering out of the snow, and barking a friendly bark at me. One paw in front of the other, he pulled himself out of the snow bank that he was in and trotted over to me.

"Clover," I repeated but in more of a statement. I realized, actually, the way that I said his name was kind of like the way that Jim said my name – like something that had been cared for and found.

I gathered my arms from the safety of my pockets and I reached them out, hoping that he would accept my motion.

He did; no wonder this family missed this pleasant puppy, and in no time at all I had a dog buried in my arms.

Clover looked up at me with big brown eyes and gave a little sneeze due to the snowflakes still lingering on his very wet nose.

It was at that moment, thirty feet in front of the store with ink, that I realized: I had nothing tying me down here. Nothing holding me back; I wasn't a tree, and if I didn't like where I was standing, why couldn't I just move?

I realized, to hell with it; I could move. If I wanted to leave, no one was stopping me. If I never wanted to come back, I didn't have to.

"We're going home, Clover," I muttered. He gave me a sloppy kiss in approval, and I turned around and walked until I arrived back at the sign, hanging on the dingy pole.

I set Clover down, pulled a pen from my coat pocket, and scrawled the address that was written on the sign down on my wrist.

"This is getting ink?" I heard from behind me.

With a small gasp, I turned and looked up at Jim.

"Oh, it's you," I said, relieved.

Jim laughed. "Don't sound so excited."

I saw my reflection in his eyes, and it was funny because I actually saw myself for the first time in a long while.

"Well, what are you supposed to be doing, Sir?" I asked back kind of sarcastically. He seemed surprised; I was too. I didn't usually respond like that. It wasn't in my repertoire of pre-practiced scripted responses, after all.

"I'm on lunch break. Heading out."

I thought about it for a second. Risks. Today was about risks. I felt safe with Clover at my feet now. His sign and him made everything in my own life feel like it was falling into place now like it too, had been on a "lost" sign and had now been found.

"Where have you always wanted to go?"

"What?" Jim's nose was starting to get pretty red.

"Where have you always wanted to go?" I repeated. "How does Boston sound?"

"Well," he stumbled, "from what I've heard... Boston sounds nice."

"Do you want to go?" My words sounded like a challenge. I don't know if I meant them to, but I wasn't used to this side of me; I wasn't used to asking these kinds of questions or any questions for that matter, and so I think that's why they sounded so foreign...

I watched Jim mull the idea over. I slightly giggled at the fact that he questioned me no more, but he seriously considered my proposition.

"You know what?" He pulled his hands out of his pockets with that statement.

I perked up. The cars rushed behind me, the people walked past us, and the commotion was muted.

"I've been considering a new job anyways. So, sure. Let's go," he agreed.

I bowed my head, glancing at my inverted toes, and smiled.

When I looked back up, Jim was smiling too, and I said, "All right then. We've got a dog to drop off to some people who care first, and then we're free to go."

We're free to go...

It didn't take long for me to start second guessing myself. "We could find a new job," I added after thinking about it and realizing that this decision was extremely uncharacteristic of me.

Jim sighed, looked me in my nervous eyes, and in the stern, but caring way that only Jim can do, boldly stated: "You're worth more than that."

Glancing back down at the ink scribbled on my wrist, I recognized the street name as being just a few blocks up the road. I coyly smiled and looked forward at the scene in front of me. After realizing that the discovery of Clover was the insight that I had needed for years, I took a deep, reassuring breath, and then I began leading Jim and Clover forward.

3.
ABSCHIED
CARLA MARIA VERDINO-SÜLLWOLD

"What am I doing here?" she asked aloud as she hoisted her overnight bag up onto the bed. The surroundings were familiar enough – the plush wing chair at the fireplace, the floral chintz bedspread and drapes, the English hunt scenes adorning the walls and the view from the window across the tall white portico and onto Freeport's busy Maine Street.

No, it was not the stately old Harraseeket Inn itself which felt strange to Maya. It was the eerie singleness of the room – the odd absence of someone to share the getaway – not just anyone – but Marius – Marius Martin, her husband, lover, soul mate, friend who should have been with her now of all days, their forty-first wedding anniversary.

But Marius was gone – the life cruelly snatched from him some months before as he exercised on the treadmill – *a sudden tightening*, as her poet cousin had described it at the memorial service. And so today when Maya and Marius would surely have been celebrating together somewhere special – Acadia perhaps – she was alone.

Well, not entirely alone, Maya conceded as she headed out to her car. She had brought Barbary and Starbuck with her for companionship and comfort. She lifted the cat carrier from the back seat, snapped the leash on the big, black bear dog, and walked back to the hotel.

When she had told her local friends her plan for the day, they had raised their eyebrows quizzically. "Are you sure," one neighbor had asked. "Won't there be too many memories?"

"I want to remember," Maya had insisted. "I want to spend time with Marius. We never said goodbye."

Once inside the hotel, the Newfoundland began busily sniffing around the room, as Maya set up a cat tent with Starbuck's bed, toys, and dishes. How many times had Marius and she gone through the same ritual in hotel rooms along the East coast while they were showing the venerable Maine Coon to Supreme Grand Champion status. The still regal "Boo," as they nicknamed him, was not a stranger to hotels or travel. He relished the attention, the treats, and the luxury. He always sought out the most comfortable spot in a room. She and Marius would joke that Starbuck would rate hotel rooms with discrimination – only five-paw accommodations such as the Harraseeket met his approval. He had been here ten years before when he had competed in the big Cat Fanciers Association show at the Portland Civic Center. As he now pranced cautiously around the room, his whiskers alert, his lynx-tipped ears pricked, he seemed to be remembering.

Only Barbary had no previous connection to the place. He had entered Maya's life on an impulse after Marius' death. He was still a big, galumphing puppy who only knew Maya without Marius – *or did he?* Sometimes Maya thought Barbary sensed a presence in the house or on the beach or in the woods, and then the dog would stand erect and give a tiny moan, his brown eyes staring into the unseen. "Ah, those eyes," Maya sighed as she patted the dog's head. "Look into his eyes, and you will see me," the medium had told her channeling Marius' voice. Maya gave a little shudder and returned to her unpacking.

She put her lingerie in the drawer and set out the black sheath dress on the bed. Silly to dress up for dinner alone in Maine, but the dress was another connection to Marius. She had worn it to their fortieth anniversary dinner in Bar Harbor last fall – such a joyous celebration! They had sipped champagne in their room overlooking Frenchman's Bay. They had watched the cruise ships' lights flicker through the slate blue haze before adjourning to the restaurant for a delectable meal. Then they had finished with a nightcap in the Blue Nose's lounge where Marius had requested the piano player to serenade his wife with Cole Porter's *So in Love*.

Maya felt the lump rise in her throat, and the tears sting sharply as she involuntarily hummed the tune:

> *Strange dear but true dear*
>
> *When I'm close to you dear –*
>
> *The stars fill the sky*
>
> *So in love with you am I.*

She stopped herself from singing but not before whispering one of the last lines: *I'm yours till I die.*

Turning abruptly, she reached for Barbary's leash. "Let's go, sweet pea. You need a walk." She scooped up Starbuck and put him in his tent for safekeeping. "We won't be long, Boo Boo." The cat merely yawned.

Barbary waved his plumed tail and led the way. Heads popped up over newspapers as they crossed the elegant lobby. Maya loved the stir Barbary always created; it often helped break the ice for conversation with strangers now that her days were filled with silence. They ambled down one side of Main Street and back up the other. Pausing to peak into the hotel gift shop, Maya's eye caught a ridiculously expensive, handsome catnip mat. For Starbuck, she decided, as she paid the cashier who kindly threw a dog biscuit into the bag as well.

The magnificent old cat was fourteen now—on borrowed time for the breed. His gait was rickety; his coat had thinned; his muscle tone had begun to atrophy, and yet he retained the look— the proud, flashing green gold eyes and the square-cut muzzle thrust forward jauntily.   Returning to the room, Maya silenced the progression of this train of thought.

"I'm going to take a swim, guys," she said aloud—a habit of rhetorically addressing her pets that had only intensified in the long, quiet months following Marius' death. "Perhaps another sign of my going crazy," she wondered, but in point of fact, she didn't really care. "Barbary, you babysit Starbuck," she commanded.

The solarium was deserted. *Just as well,* thought Maya. The late afternoon sun streaming through the glass was hypnotic. She waded into the heated turquoise water and swam a few laps, then turned on her back and just floated.   Her eyes closed, she felt herself buoyed up by an unseen pair of arms—Marius', as he had so often supported her when they swam together.   The water rocked her gently into a meditative lull.

Her random thoughts meandered back to an article she had read that morning in *The Newf Tide* about Rigel, the Newfoundland hero of the Titanic, who had swum in the freezing North Atlantic waters for three hours, first searching for his drowned master, and then circling a lifeboat while barking for help until the rescue ship *Carpathian* arrived. *Amazing creatures,* she thought, flipping over and swimming to the ladder. She was glad she had not come to the Harraseeket alone, after all.

Dinner passed more quickly and pleasantly than she had imagined it would. The innkeeper, a spirited octogenarian, was making hostess rounds, and when she discovered that it had been Maya and Marius' anniversary custom to dine here, she promptly sat down and had sent over a round of complimentary cocktails. The two women found they had a surprising number of things in common, and drinks had segued into dinner. It was late when Maya found herself thanking the woman profusely for her kindness and hurrying off to her room.

After a quick walk with Barbary and changing into her nightdress, Maya liberated Starbuck from his tent and placed the brand new catnip mat on the other pillow of the king-sized bed. Magnetically drawn, Starbuck pounced onto the bed and with a flourish settled himself on the mat. Not to be outdone, Barbary hauled himself up and plopped his huge frame down across the folded quilt at the foot of the bed.

Despite the double martini, Maya didn't yet feel sleepy so she reached for the remote and flipped through channels. *Great Performances* was airing a concert from the Vienna Philharmonic, and there she stopped her search. Muti had just taken the podium with baritone Thomas Hampson. The breathtaking silence was followed by the haunting melancholy strains of Mahler. Maya closed her eyes and settled against the pillows as the last movement of *Das Lied von der Erde* washed over her. *Der Abschied—the farewell- Letzten Lebewohl—I want to bid him a last farewell.*

Tears began to fall silently down her cheeks as Starbuck's rhythmic purring harmonized with the singer's sorrow: *You leave me long alone!* Absently, her hand reached out to caress the frail, bony frame. *How soon before Starbuck, too, will be gone?* This evening, this crazy evening at the hotel was just one more goodbye. Or perhaps, it was not a new parting, but only the same long, leave-taking, a continuum of the one she never had gotten to utter to Marius – an opportunity to rewrite the last act, to erase regret, to say all the things that should be said before the abyss engulfed her, too.

She bent down and planted a kiss on the old cat's head, and nonplussed, Starbuck yawned and languidly stretched out a paw – a sovereign demanding homage. Barbary, sensing Maya's need, lumbered up to lick her face before inserting himself between his mistress and the cat. Starbuck leaned into the warm, luxurious fur and curled himself contentedly against Barbary's chest. With a sigh, Maya let herself collapse into the heap of snoring, purring fur and clung to the contented creatures as if they were a life raft. This was her rescue! Like Rigel, Barbary was plucking her from the surging torrents of grief.

Ewig – forever – ewig.   The singer's fading lament seemed to link together the goodbyes of the past with the imminent ones ahead. For Maya, time was a tortuous thread. But for Starbuck and Barbary, there was no thought of eternity – only the blessedness of this moment.

4.
AFTER THE DIFFICULTIES
MADELYN D. KAMEN

Everyone said they were a cute couple. Many knew she was a bit older than he was and could see she was a few inches taller. But no one seemed to care about those superficial things these days. *Compatibility* was the magic word.

They had such fun together. They liked the same foods, the same sports, even the same people. And they found a place to settle in, just big enough for two. They found it warm and cozy and out of the way. A place to retire when the whole world seemed too much for them. And close enough to the park that they could take long walks or just sit by the picnic tables under the trees and breathe in the fresh air. As the Gerswin song says, *Summertime and the living is easy.*

What could go wrong in a situation like this? KIDS!!

Everything went well until the kids came along. She had them 1, 2, 3, 4, one after the other. He stood by the crib as each new denizen joined the family and took over some of their care and education. People may have been surprised at his efforts at domestic life, but they never expected the kids to be more in his domain than hers. When she was through with them for the day, she merely stood, shook her body and hair, and went about her everyday business. Then he took over.

Now, the cozy little place they had been staying seemed cramped and uncomfortable. At first, each parent tried to be accommodating, leaving the sleeping area for their spouse and the children and finding a not so ideal place to sleep themselves. They shared most of their food with their spouse and the children.

But, the problem was greater than people imagined. In a word, the doctor diagnosed it as a proclivity for sex of all kinds and matches. It seemed that the whole family was open-minded about sexual partners. The males with females, no matter the relationship; the females with males. And same-sex kin with each other.

The doctor explained their affliction was natural as daylight. But, if they were upset, he had a remedy for their non-stop peccadilloes. He took each of the family members one by one—on six different days and in six different weeks into his operating room and cured them.

A few months after his work was done, the doctor asked the family into his conference room so that he might do a follow-up. One-by-one he asked them how satisfied they were with the procedures he had performed on each of them.

And one-by-one they answered the same thing: woof, woof, woof, woof, woof, woof.

5.
AGAPAO
JOHN C. MANNONE

How unreal it is to have unconditional love.
I read the Bible, go to church, try
to love my neighbor, even when he's a jerk
but sometimes I just don't feel like it.

And when fast isn't fast enough while driving
down the highway, and some SUV is breathing
on my bumper, it's hard to show a brotherly love
of patience for the ignorant, let alone show a deep
sense of forgiveness, especially when the driver
nearly sideswipes me in a road-rage maneuver,
fingers flying from both hands.

When they executed Timothy McVeigh
for the Oklahoma City bombing, I rejoiced,
but much to my surprise, the Book of Numbers
was keeping a different kind of score. I wasn't
supposed to have reveled when they stopped
his heart with potassium chloride. But I did.

And when I, in my too-busy schedule, would forget
to hug my Max, spend a little more time with him
after being gone for hours or not leave him out
in the cold when the air was bittered with ice
and I didn't bring him in, he didn't hold it against me.

Instead, he'd spring straight-up on all fours in joy,
a one-hundred pound "fur covered jumping bean,"
Max, always thankful at my coming home.

Now, when I read the good Book and see that
I'm to go out into all the world and make disciples
of men, teaching them, I learned how to do that,
I learned that some dogs must be God's disciples.
Max was one of them.

6.
BELLA THE BUTTER EATING BORDER COLLIE
PHILIPPE SHILS

Amanda told me as she left
to take Lucia to school:

You have to put the butter
away. Bella eats the butter.
But I put it on
the window sill.
No. Yesterday. Bella ate the butter.
And the butter isn't on the window
sill today. It's on the
butcher block.
I was on the porch.
Felix was in his high chair.

The butter.
Where was the butter?

BELLA THE BUTTER EATING
BORDER COLLIE
PHILIPPE SHILS

7.
BISCUITS
JOHN C. MANNONE

Max loved to eat cat
-head biscuits at the Sweetwater
Motel where we found him. A truck
driver fed him biscuits everyday
outside his courtyard room.
My wife and I watched the dog
through the restaurant window,
his methodical search patterns
left no shrub-dirt uninspected
for food someone might have placed there.

Only a two-month-old collie,
shaggy black with a white diamond
on his nose, but already showing signs
of remarkable intelligence
and survival skills. In the motel
restaurant at a nearby table,
the trucker, seeing us look
at the dog, sensed our compassion.
He asked, "Do you want him?
He's just a stray I've fed, but
I got to hit the road. I named him Max."

I've forgotten why Max, maybe because
the name reminded him of his Scottish
ancestry, the clear cool springs
of mountains, like the Smokies here.

I stared back
with that thanks-but-no-thanks look.
Max raised his eyes by the door
from the courtyard. We said we couldn't
leave him, not with a serious infection.
His white chest fur streaked red.

So we took him
to the Vet's; planned to find
a home for him. Max shivered,
his teeth rattling against each other
as we took him away
from the only home he ever knew.
I fetched the napkin-wrapped
biscuit I had slipped in my pocket.
Offered it to Max. I spoke
a language he did not know
but understood the tone. And his
eyes spoke one I understood.
We finally found him a home,
ours.

8.
BORN INTOLERANT
A.J. HUFFMAN

I give my Chihuahua occasional scraps
of gristle I cut from my steak
because he was born intolerant
to red meat, and even the smallest piece
of hamburger makes him sick. The residual
flavor of the fat fools his mind and taste buds.
He smiles and pants, licks me on the cheek
for granting him reprieve
from his bland diet of specially formulated
dog food. For one elicit moment he is free,
a reincarnation of feral ancestor, savoring
the taste of victory torn from captured prey.

9.
BROWN DOG
ELIZABETH MCMUNN-TETANGCO

I didn't see how he arrived—

His small brown shape taut

As the handle of a knife

—Or how he left.

I think of him, sleeping in

The yellow field, his heartbeat

Counting stars.

10.
COUPLING
RICK BLUM

He lies on the couch, head nuzzled in her lap
while she knits a blanket or, perhaps, a sweater
he'll wear when the mercury crashes. He'll stay as long
as it takes, listening to the soft clickety-click lullaby

of darting needles, drifting in and out of consciousness
till her spring unwinds deep in the enveloping night.
Earlier they walked, never more than a few yards apart,
like a pair of doves in a cozy, dome-top cage. Sometimes,

when she tells him of her repressed desires, crushing
disappointments, unrealized dreams, he'll cock his head
to look at her with inquisitive, brown eyes that say
"Tell me all" – just the gesture she needs to keep

moving forward toward an indiscernible horizon.
When they return, she makes him dinner, lovingly
mixing savory chicken with hand-chopped veggies –
the way he likes it best. Later, when she's lying in bed

shaped like a backward *S*, arms pulled in close
to her chest, he'll squeeze into the small space between
her head and knees, give a barely audible sigh, then
match her soft breath for soft breath 'til the first shafts

of light creep in past a raggedy window shade. That's
when I roll over, drape my arm over her silky waist,
and let my hand rest gently on his curly-coated haunch –
coupling the three of us for one more day.

11.
DOG IN WINTER
HUGH ANDERSON

The cold has trapped her too long
sprawled on the hearth rug, twitching
and yipping in squirrel filled dreaming.
Though I am loath to abandon my book
and easy chair, I uncloset her leash
and dance her excitement out the door.

Something about frozen ground
and print-pocked snow must capture,
scent, for though she pulls
for the familiar destination, each post,
each tree, each clump of icy grass
demands she sniff its story to the end.

Finally, the hundred stairs, the beach.
The sky is glass, cold sun a distant beam
shot through it. Freed from her leash,
she skates across the springs that slide
across the sand and freeze below
the ice-fanged bluffs. She starts at seaweed
frozen as it tumbled from a windy tide, half-crisp,
its salt still liquid, its water turned ice.

Where the salt is thicker and the tide
just ebbed, the sand is soft and ridged
with echoes of the recent waves. Here
the dog stops sniffing shore stories and runs
full of the energy of space, of earth that gives
when her paws push down, sprays generously
when she leans into a high speed turn. Her tail
is a flag of joy, her breath bursts out in clouds.
She stops and faces the wind.

The sky is crystal, the earth rock.
Here in this half land of recent sea,
she is ancient and unleashed.

12.
DOG RUN
ELIZABETH WARD

Look at those two, having such a lark!
Noses to ground, then inhaling the north wind,
Fetching the scent of snow from across the lake,
They chase each other through fields and tangled borders,
      not in play
But that one might not miss the other's find.

I know why they're excited.
It's not my senses outplaying theirs,
      but the simple fact I cheat.
On horseback I can view their future
      while they run down the past.

That big coyote hunting mice,
      there,
      head down in thick grass,
Will sense us soon and run.
He didn't when first he saw me
      some week or two ago,
But stood agog at the two-headed beast
      my pony and I make.

Then he spied the dogs,
      the smaller one almost his size,
      the other twice as large,
And took off for the trees.
Now he knows I've back-up;
      he doesn't stop to watch,
But disappears in autumn cornrows
      that match him brown and gray.

Had he the sense of humor
　　　I've seen our foxes show,
He'd double back to watch,
　　　enjoy with me this sight:

The gray dog and the brown
　　　still circling meadows at top speed,
Searching for this moment.

Previous publication in the chapbook Naked Weimaraner: The Dogs,
The Cats, The Rest, Shaggy Dog Press, 2005

13.
DOGGIE PERSONALS
GARY BECK

Winter had left a tarpaulin of sooty snow covering the city. Few of the local dog owners risked braving the elements at Tompkins Square Park. *Had their dogs mastered indoor plumbing?* But it was a blessing for me and my dog. Pard's sexual impulses had alienated my fellow dog walkers in the park, so our absence from the regular dog walking sessions for the last few months had not been lamented. Now that harsh nature ruled the land, yuppies, and their pampered pooches were in hibernation. The rigors of the Iditarod to the park were only to be dared by the dauntless. By the time the weather improved, Pard's crass despoliation of a Pomeranian would mostly be forgotten, except by the violated owner and the wuss who championed her. But they were probably skulking in the cave. The park was ours for the moment, at least that's what our foot and paw prints, and the yellow stains of Pard's urine on the blackened snowdrifts indicated. I found myself wondering: *Was yellow on a field of black the colors of the Viet Cong flag? The Pittsburg Penguins hockey team?* I didn't see any of the park's homeless population. *Did they freeze to death and get buried in the snow drifts? Was Pard urinating on their graves?* I guess my frivolity was due to our unexpectedly pleasant romp in the park.

Perhaps the cold weather had dampened Pard's sexual ardor, although it hadn't affected mine. I knew his urges would recur in the spring and I hadn't forgotten my vow to help him. Our summer campaign for doggie sex had ended in exile to Elba. *Was St. Helena in our future?* But I refused to give up hope. I had tried various ways to get Pard... *Why couldn't I find a comfortable phrase?* Man's crudity in describing the sexual act was distressing. Did you ever hear an intelligent woman say: "I got my ashes hauled." Or, "I jumped his bones?" Though isn't it ironic that so many women, in the excesses of freedom, had become as vulgar as men? It is an inherent human right to be as stupid as anyone else, but it's preferable to ascend the intelligence scale, rather than stampede to a lower common denominator.

I had exhausted my meager resources in the struggle to fulfill Pard's sexual needs. I would never again call my ex-girlfriend, Anitra, the flighty painter, who was a fountain, a geyser, a cascade, a veritable Niagara of smug, gloating, useless advice. We were on our own again, lone wolves fending for ourselves in a hostile environment. I decided that we would never again lurk in sexual ambush, or beg, plead, cajole, pester, or offer bribes for sexual favors. I also determined not to indulge in fantasies. They hadn't solved any problems and they only diverted me from my purpose. My thoughts kept coming back to not being able to find any information about doggie sex. It seemed ridiculous that in the information age there could be such a void, especially since the smut and porno activity on the World Wide Web was becoming pandemic. I was astonished that so many creeps, sickos, and social detriti had grasped the significance of the Internet. *Ah, the blessings of democracy, for every freedom an abuse.* Then, before I got carried away by ineffectual socio-political musings, an idea floated into mind. *I could start a newsletter for dog owners and include a personals section that might help find a female for Pard.*

My first chore was to assure myself that this wasn't a fantasy. Therefore, I needed a plan. I started by organizing my thoughts and reviewing the situation. The purpose of the newsletter would be to locate a dog owner who would make a female available for sex with Pard. The newsletter would obviously have to be respectable, or it would attract every weirdo, psycho, macho nut in the western hemisphere. A combination of creative writing and desktop publishing should produce an acceptable publication. It needn't make money though I could charge for personals if someone would pay for them. The newsletter would have to exist long enough for Pard to meet the bitch of his dreams. If the newsletter was a monthly, three or four issues might do the trick. *I could do that!* The creative part seemed easy, even fun. Distribution required some thought, for in order for the newsletter to be effective, it would have to reach, and then influence a receptive dog owner, who would then respond favorably to an ad. This would be a true challenge since I really wasn't much of an entrepreneur. *Did Hearst say that when he first started peddling papers?*

I sketched out an outline of the newsletter and made notes for what I needed to make it functional. I could write and publish it at my apartment, but I needed a phone number and mailing address for inquiries. I knew I couldn't use my home number, or I might have to deal with the legions of the demented, so I'd have to get a telephone service and a temporary postal box. *What was I forgetting? Could it be this easy to do a newsletter?* Maybe. After all, my need wasn't as great as Tom Paine's. I went back to the problem of distribution. I decided that I could leave copies at the Tompkins Square Park dog run in good weather and the coffee shops, bars and restaurants in the east village were good sites. This wasn't a bad beginning. Then I got a flash of inspiration. I could mail copies to the cable talk shows with a promotional letter. They might think it an interesting or entertaining topic and give the newsletter coverage. There was no good reason not to go out of the neighborhood. My new motto could be: 'Have horny pooch. Will travel.'

The content of the first issue would include: a rewritten article about pampered pooches that I could borrow from a recent news story; humorous or zany letters to the editor that I would write; a how-to article; e.g. 'How to sneak your dog past customs in Athens, Greece'; shoppers tips (wild game dog food and retro clothing selections); and personals, lots and lots of personals. I was obviously going to be busy for a while, but this project might be more constructive than my previous furtive solicitations for a sex partner for Pard. It was fun so far and the writing would be a blast. I could say anything. Well, almost anything. I couldn't lose sight of my objective, a hot date for Pard. Then new concerns hit me. Did I have to prepare him in any way? Special grooming? A scented bath? A new collar? Doggie condoms? Should he bring flowers? Was there a well-defined protocol for these get-togethers, or would I have to invent one? I made a note to go on the internet and find out how animal stud procedures were handled. Maybe I could pick up a few pointers.

The immediate results of my decision to publish 'The Doggie Tribune' were encouraging. There was a new buoyancy in my step. My acting students at Gotham University's School of the Arts once again got the attention that they were expensively paying for. Well, that mommy and daddy were paying for. My department chairman, 'Ernest the emoter' stopped hounding me about my poor attitude. He even hinted that he might let me direct a student production next semester if I applied the requisite amount of lip to the designated orifice. My grin didn't waver though my thoughts were homicidal. The prospect of directing the thespian primates wasn't alluring. I concealed my distaste, put on an obsessed expression and mumbled: "Thanks, Ernie. I'd like to direct a Jacobean tragedy. Something with blood, gore, sex, violence, incest, and necrophilia. It should also be in rhymed verse. I'll do some research and get back to you." He gaped at me as if I was mad, loco, nuts, gaga, bonkers, off the wall. I smiled diabolically. "Think about it, Ernie." Again using the slang name he hated. I jauntily waved goodbye and fled the factory confines of the university that were as oppressive to me as George III's institutions were to the rowdy Sons of Liberty.

Home life was also much improved. My current girlfriend had no complaints and was content with our casual relationship. She kept referring to the interesting women she met at a gay bar, but that didn't bother me. *Why should competition from a woman be any worse than from a man?* Pard was more relaxed. With the subsidence of his sexual tensions, his constant howling when I was away ceased. This temporarily disarmed the landlord, who would now have to seek another *causus belli* to remove me. So with tranquility at home and stability on the frontiers, I turned my energies to yellow journalism. I'd make Jonathan Swift proud of me. Well, he might at least smile or snicker if I was witty enough. I knew there were no Pulitzers in my future, no glamorous foreign assignments, no fame, no fortune, no respect from my peers. However, there was a real possibility that I might fulfill my faithful doggie's needs.

I efficiently laid out one sheet and folded it into a four-page format, with a section for a bold masthead 'The Doggie Tribune', Vol. I. December, 1999. The first page would have an editorial titled: 'Entertainment for your dog when you go to work'. I recommended playing music reflecting the owner's taste, to divert the dog from feelings of loneliness. For the bottom of page one, I created an ad for space-age dog boots that allowed the dog to handle the most demanding weather conditions. I included a short testimonial by the NASA animal trainer, who swore he'd send his dog to Mars in these boots. Page two would have a how-to article: 'Training your dog at home by audio tape, while you're away, at work, or at play'. Customized tapes covered various training sequences. My favorite was 'How to keep your dog off the bed'. I had to laugh since Pard used the bed almost as much as I did and I could never break him of that habit.

Page three would be devoted to reader's letters. I quickly wrote several. One was from an attorney specializing in animal law. He advocated passing a constitutional amendment guaranteeing animal rights. Another was from a San Francisco politician who wanted to change city ordinances to include the term 'pet guardian', when referring to animal-people relationships. He asserted that this would undermine the idea that animals were human property. It would also reduce violence against animals by reminding humans that they were guardians, not owners. The first three pages took me less than an hour and I was ready for the real goal, the personals column. I used the sleaze column of 'The Village Tonsil' as my guide and listed various categories: write to me/personals; females seeking males; males seeking females; multiples; anything goes. I tried to be reasonably sedate in the first issue, but got carried away with the 'anything goes' category. I wrote: 'Male Golden Retriever seeks small, light coated female for golden showers.' I cackled over that and giggled uncontrollably at: 'Single female Doberman seeks paw lover with oral skills'.

I had strayed far from serious composition by the time I finished multiples: 'Lusty male Airedale seeks male Collies, or other medium sized purebred males, to form a pack to pursue bitches in heat. Papers required.' I forced myself to get back to male seeks female. I tried three different approaches, each meant for Pard. I thought the most promising was: 'Hirsute male seeks sensitive female for companionship and fun. No body piercing.' Well, the great experiment was underway. Peter Zenger certainly started with less. I ran spellcheck, double checked for typos, instructed my obedient machine, pushed print and out came the first edition of 'The Doggie Tribune'. I yelled "Stop the presses" and reviewed the result. It didn't look bad at all. I made some notes for revision, slightly changed the layout, added some decorative elements: separation lines and sidebars, and verified that there was enough room for address, phone number, and box numbers, once I got them. As a writer, I was not dissatisfied. As a publisher, I was happy. Soon I would be a delivery boy. I never had a paper route when I was a kid so this might be an adventure.

I was very busy for the next few days. I got a telephone service and opened a postal box. These vital production tools obtained, I finalized the newsletter by putting in address and phone number, and went to press. I printed until I ran out of paper, then I folded until my fingers got stiff. I had more than three hundred copies for the delivery boy, me. Now all that remained was to get the paper on the streets, sit back and await replies. I toured the east village, discreetly placing copies in 'in' spots. As I walked, I kept finding new locations: The Tompkins Square Library, the Theater for the New City lobby, bulletin boards in laundromats and veterinarian offices, and some of the pretentious food shops on 1st Avenue. By the end of the first day of newspaper delivery, I was pleased by my discovery of new sites, each one potentially able to bring a sex partner to Pard. *What if he got a lot of responses? Would he be able to handle the demand? Should I put him in training? Start him on a special diet? Get pep pills?* Well, I had a lot to think about.

The reward for action is happiness, however fleeting. I went to school with a feeling of well-being that wasn't easily discouraged by the uninspired efforts of my acting students. I didn't even mind that fewer and fewer female students flirted with me. Not that I ever responded, but as a practicing male it wasn't unpleasant to look at the class and see flirtatious eyes and alluring thighs. The decline of student-teacher enticement was probably due to the latest Gotham U. trend, female students mating with other female students. I agree that it's safer, saner and subtler, but what a joke on mommy and daddy, who were spending upwards of fifty Gs per annum, for their beloved daughter to find the pleasures of the flesh in the arms of another woman. It would take a few more years until parents became aware of the true nature of the roommate. But it wasn't my concern. If young men were more functional and reassuring, there would probably be fewer mass female defections from the traditional male/female roles. If a woman was more capable than a man, why shouldn't she get the girl?

Despite diverse competition, my new girlfriend was still happy with me. Judy Ching was a Chinese-American, whose family immigrated when comrade Mao and his merry men concluded the long march into Peking, in 1947. Judy was the third generation fortified by ample American protein. She was tall, muscular, athletic, yet feminine. We met in an internet café. After careful screening to verify that I wasn't a serial killer or an oriental slaver with a customer in mind, we saw each other often. Judy was a computer programmer and worked as a webmaster for a company that distributed sexual paraphernalia. Despite her professional and amateur interest in sex, Judy wasn't sympathetic to my efforts to find a sex partner for Pard. However, she compensated for this by not minding that I thought of her as mysterious and exotic, although she was a virtual throwback to small town Americana values, having been nurtured by a doting family. She even was amused by my sense of humor, which usually alienated everyone. This became clear to me after the first time we made love. She tenderly asked: "How was it?" and wasn't the least bit offended when I enthusiastically replied: "Ding Hao, baby."

So the only serpent in our Shangri-La was what she called my obsession with Pard's sexual needs. Judy loved Pard. He had always been friendly to my girlfriends, but he liked her from the start and won her over with his best look of total adoration. She fell under his spell, fed him dog treats, brushed him, which I generally neglected and thought it was cute that he ate all our leftovers. She even took him for walks and coped well with the hazards of dog walking in the city. But she refused to endorse my activities on behalf of Pard's need. She thought it was tacky.

"You just have to be patient. It will work out."

"Yeah. Right. Tell that to Pard when his scrotum's aching."

"There's no need to be crude," she said frostily. This issue was a source of growing friction between us, until the wonderful day of her conversion.

Judy had trained Pard to do tricks like fetch, meditate—she actually got him to sit on his haunches, front paws crossed, eyes closed, and mumblegrowlpurr or something. I laughed every time I saw him in that ridiculous pose. She stalwartly defended him, asserting that he was seeking enlightenment, which would insure his rebirth on a higher plane.

"I didn't know you were a Buddhist?"

"I'm not. We're some kind of Episcopalians though I could never figure out exactly what that meant. I just love the idea of transmigration of souls."

I wisely – for once – refrained from a smart-ass remark and as if there was justice in the universe, I was rewarded for my discretion. Judy had taught Pard to walk on his hind legs. One evening she decided to teach him to dance. I made the standard macho objections but was overruled and sent to the sidelines, mumbling ineffectually: "Next you'll make him wear a tutu."

Then it happened. They were practicing the fox trot and he was doing so well that she hugged him. He hugged back and suddenly he was humping her leg. Out of its sheath popped his red, shiny thing, rubbing against her. She tried to push him down, but he growled fiercely, scaring her and clasped her tightly, scratching her with his claws. I responded instantly to her cries for help and removed the vile malefactor, who hadn't had time to ejaculate, but managed to leak some fluid on her leg. I took her to the bathroom, gently wiped his emission, tenderly laved her wounds with peroxide and emanated the utmost sympathy for her traumatic experience. After all, attempted rape is unsettling. I continued to suppress all wisecracks though temptation wriggled and jiggled inside me. "I don't understand. He never did anything like that before," she said.

I burst out laughing until I saw her indignant look. "Sorry."

"What's so funny?" she asked ominously.

"I remembered that line from a joke."

"Tell me." I felt the sands shifting 'neath my feet.

"Another time, when you're more relaxed." She was implacable.

"Tell me."

"A man took his dog to a bar and ordered a beer. The bartender asked jokingly: 'What'll the pooch have?' The dog said: 'I'll have a beer.' The bartender was surprised and turned to the man. 'You're a ventriloquist, right?' 'No, this is a genuine talking dog.' The bartender got excited. 'There's a newsstand around the corner and the owner and I have been playing tricks on each other for years. Give your dog this dollar and have him go to the newsstand and buy a paper.' The man agreed and sent the dog off. Time went by; the dog didn't come back, the man got worried and went to look for him. The newsstand owner thought he was crazy when he asked him if he saw his talking dog, so he scoured the neighborhood, calling: 'Here, Arnold. Here, Arnold.' He saw movement in an alley, looked closer and saw Arnold mounted on a nondescript female, doggying away. He yelled: 'Arnold you never did anything like that before.' Arnold looked around and said: 'I never had any money before.'"

Judy glared, the thousand cuts that her ancestors favored flashed from her eyes, and then she dissolved into laughter. Perhaps the serenity of our garden of earthly delights was saved. "You are just like your dog."

Uh, oh. Were we being indicted for horniness? "Actually, I came first, so he would be like me."

She leaped up, grabbed me by the ears and kissed me. Just as I was introducing some tongue to the act, she pulled away.

"Don't quibble. I understand now what you've been trying to tell me."

Was this the triumph of the theory that a big, stiff one speaks louder than words? But far be it for me to question this fortuitous turnabout. Judy had finally realized that I wasn't a perverse monster, pandering to an artificially concocted need. Now all that remained was to enlist her considerable intellect in my campaign for doggie sex for Pard.

Judy came through like the Chi-coms storming into Korea. She took photos of Pard in various poses. Then she took another series of photos with Pard wearing bikini underwear, a leather vest and shades, vinyl hot pants and a large codpiece. The results were either suggestive or downright pornographic. She showed the photos to her employer, the distributor of sexual paraphernalia and he went wild for the concept of a sex symbol dog. He immediately offered Pard a modeling contract, which I had to approve as his legal guardian. Of course, I played cool and agreed to let my lawyer review the terms, but inside I was happily rapping because I knew celebrities got plenty of... Well, you know what I mean. I still hadn't found a couth phrase to describe the acquisition of sexual favors. For a glorious moment, I succumbed to fantasy and pictured Pard besieged by bevies of beautiful bitches, wagging to serve him. Then I remembered my anti-fantasy vow and compelled myself back to what had become promising reality. Besides, the unexpected money didn't hurt either. It wouldn't allow me to retire in luxury, but it would keep Pard in dog biscuits for a long, long time.

So all was well for a fleeting moment, but I should have realized that this was not meant to be, since I was neither virtuous enough nor wise enough to attain happiness. Then, as if destiny prepared my downfall, every recent success began to unravel. Judy's boss, the distributor of sexual paraphernalia, decided that a dog wasn't the appropriate representative of a line of products for humans and he withdrew the contract offer. Judy got more and more involved with a woman she met in a chat room, and saw less and less of me. She also stopped her efforts in the search for a sex partner for Pard, further adding to our frustration. The newsletter that I thought was so clever generated no response. Zero, zip, zilch, nada, nil, naught. It's not that the endeavor was a wasteful expenditure of resources as if I had other options, but I will admit that expectations had possessed me. Pard moped without Judy and howled piteously during the day, provoking the landlord to threaten another round of legal action.

Then school became a trouble spot. I was short tempered with my acting students and they sulked or whined, but of course didn't rebel, since I had the power of the grade. Nothing was more important to them than achieving the highest possible grade. The student herd had been completely taken in by the system and had renounced independent thought, dropped all resistance to unsettling ideas, and placed learning in a subsidiary role to getting along. Unless the school caught me on a morals charge, or in a drug bust, the students had to take my crap. If I fell from my not too lofty perch, the herd would turn on me in an instant and trample me under their hooves. And as if I wasn't burdened enough, 'Ernest the emoter' approved my directing a student production. Not an obscure Jacobean monster that would stupefy Cromwell himself, but a nice musical, or a sedate Neil Simon comedy. "Yeah. Right."

So the promise of a mere few weeks ago that happiness was at hand, or right around the corner, was just another deception. However, I was stronger than I used to be and refused to wallow in misery. Well, at least most of the time. I disciplined myself not to take my frustration out on my students, no matter how much they were entitled to suffer for their art. I urged 'Ernest the emoter' to let me do an O'Neill or Inge play, something American, but with substance. He was dubious, but reluctantly agreed to consider my revolutionary selection. Judy was just about lost to me. I couldn't help wondering if my crude jokes—she hated the one about the coolie's daughter—and my teasing her for not having bound feet contributed to her departure. The one good thing that came out of the newsletter was that I followed my own advice and left the radio on the classical station at home and Pard stopped howling. This would at least postpone the inevitable conflict with the landlord.

Now, if I could only find a solution to Pard's sexual needs before the passions of spring drove him mad, it might not be the best of all possible worlds, but it would at least be temporarily acceptable.

14.
DOGS HOWL IN MONSOONS
NANCY J. SHATTUCK

"Dogs howl during monsoons?" Dr. Shelly Walker jabbed the syringe needle into the serum and injected the dog for rabies. Before he could answer, Anil, who volunteered at the Kalimpong Veterinary Clinic, bolted out of the room to answer the phone.

Shelly, also a volunteer, swept a hank of fine brown hair off her forehead as she watched him go. Though slight, she was tall and had to bend as she examined the anesthetized dog on the stainless steel table. A black saddle marking a mottled gray coat and a nervous bark: this one was "Yak." *A talker*, she thought. Though Asian street dogs all stood within inches of the same height, a triumph of natural selection, they retained more identifying marks and distinctive personalities than breed dogs did. Recognizing that, Shelly named each stray that came into the clinic.

She adjusted her wire-frame glasses, but as she began to prepare the castration site, Anil returned. The native of Kalimpong bustled to the operating table. "A dog's been injured," he said.

"They will bring the dog here?"

He shook his head. "He said, he can't move it..."

Shelly cut him off. "Did you tell him we only treat large animals at an injury site?"

Anil lifted both hands, wagged them, signaling his distress. "I did," he said. "But it's N.J."

She groaned. Everyone in Kalimpong knew N.J. so well they referred to him by his initials. Head of the Darjeeling Health Ministry, he could shut the clinic down if they refused him.

Usually, there were two vets on duty, but her partner, the resident Dr. Suddha Shivaji, was in nearby Darjeeling for the week. "Where's the dog?" She hoped it was not a long Jeep ride through the Himalayas.

"It's at his house, Mountain View, the one at the top. You haven't started operating yet. I can get this dog back in its cage."

"That's Yak!" she snapped. "He has a name."

"*Yak's* cage, then." Anil responded.

Shelly removed her rubber gloves. Relenting, she said, "I'm sorry, I haven't been sleeping."

Anil scooped up the limp dog in his arms, talking over his shoulder as he moved toward the cages. "The howling?" he asked.

"They've woken me every night for the last week!" Shelly assembled her medicine bag. *More gauze and tape*, she thought, turning to the supply cabinet.

"It's the monsoons," Anil said. "But for one month only."

"Does anyone sleep?" she asked. Anil, intent on securing the anesthetized dog in the cage, grunted for an answer.

Shelly was proud of the clinic's mission to rescue street dogs when most communities exterminated them. Despite the monotony of her work (testing, rabies vaccination, neutering, ear notch and tattoo), she believed in what she did. Released back to the streets, the stray dogs posed no hazard to humans; in fact, the packs that roamed were a benefit, as they controlled the rat population. The Indian government had outfitted this clinic as a test site to see if the process could control both the rabies and plague diseases. She had fought with her fiancé, Mark, over volunteering for the six-month position as veterinarian on graduating from the University. She'd tried to explain to him that she was interested in this experimental clinic because it researched disease control. Mark, a veterinarian too, had finally relented and she had come to Kalimpong, an isolated Himalayan town of only forty thousand residents.

Small animals were not her favorite work. Mark loved working with pets, but her joy was working with large animals, or, barring that, farm and community programs that benefited large populations. Her interests were more academic than Mark's, who sought the security of a sure income from his small animal hospital.

Shelly's only concession to pets in Kalimpong had been to accept free board and room at the charming Himalaya Hotel in exchange for care of the owner's two Pekingese dogs. The compromise comprised a love of air conditioning and a latent romantic streak. The hotel was over-the-top romantic.

Leaving the clinic, she didn't stop to say hello to Shiva, a tan street dog that adopted the sidewalk in front of the clinic as home. Shiva raised an eyelid but didn't lift his head from his paws as she passed. *Probably sleeping off his night,* she thought. *Too bad I can't.*

****

It was dark when Shelly returned to the clinic. The dog, Orchid, had been seriously injured by a car, and she had treated broken ribs, chest lacerations and a compound fracture of its leg. She would check on her in the morning, but the prognosis was not good. If the chest wound became infected, Orchid wouldn't survive. Often, small animals drowned in their own chest fluids in such cases.

The clinic was just half a mile below the Himalaya Hotel, and she walked home through streets lined by gated estates. Hungrier than usual because she had worked through lunch, she realized it would be more than an hour before the hotel served dinner. She considered going to the Fresh Bite restaurant but decided she was too tired. On days when she was homesick, she walked down to Fresh Bite, where the owner had a passion for American music and his prodigious collection of pop music spanned more than fifty years.

Shelly always felt a calm spread through her when she walked under the arched gateway into the gardens of the Himalaya Hotel. She was convinced that the gardener, a dark, silent wraith, communed with nature spirits to create such harmony. His established gardens were a glory of color and forms tucked in bamboo, rhododendron and azalea groves. She so wanted Mark to visit her here, but he remained unresolved on joining her for two weeks.

She climbed the stone path in the dark, following the sound of the water trickling from a bamboo pipe to a stone basin below it. At her door, the cascade of bougainvillea brushed her hands as she entered the modern wing. There, she took a hot shower and swathed in a sheet towel, napped before dinner.

****

She and Mark had met in an anatomy class. Both struggled with the class and soon after meeting, decided two heads were better than one. Mark was just two inches taller than she was, with dark brown hair and hazel eyes. His build hinted that he might someday battle his weight though his active occupation ruled out the probability. Oddly, long, thick eyelashes made his eyes his most prominent feature. Shelly was smitten when they faced each other across a library table where they studied for the first exam.

From the beginning, she had not doubted Mark. Intensely romantic, she assumed his feelings were mutual. When their initial passion cooled during their years in school, neither felt that anything was missing. Their studies and career filled the blank with a profoundly close friendship. They worked well together and Shelly never questioned they would marry.

She admired Mark because he knew exactly what he wanted in life. After he finished school, he planned to marry and start a family. Having been an only child, he wanted three children, maybe more. He knew by the time he was eighteen what Shelly did not. Her plans were vague and often, life rolled out before her like a yellow brick road. Her admiration for Mark spilled over to acceptance of his plans as reasonable for her own, with very few exceptions.

When she and Mark had argued, Shelly's desire to travel was often the cause. When she first voiced her strong desire to travel to the Potala Palace and Machu Pichu, Mark reacted with alarm. It became clear that he associated traveling women with unsavory character. He joked about hippies and hiker girls. She retorted that "woman" plus "travel" does not equal "tramp." Maybe men traveled for sexual adventure, but women do not, she assured him. She wanted to marry, have a home and family, and also travel. In the end, Mark said he was willing to compromise on vacations. He agreed that two weeks each year, they would travel to any place that she wanted to go.

****

Though Shelly's room was spotless and tastefully decorated with modern platform bed and chairs, it lacked the charm of the main house where she ate her meals most nights. She loved the English chintz of the furnishings there; wide, long verandas, dark plank flooring, and cozy cushioned reading nooks resplendent with Chinese and Tibetan rugs, and tapestries.

At dinner, she nodded to the young couple who sat at the next table in the near-empty dining room. She loved to talk to travelers, but with the start of monsoons, very few came now.

"Are you American?" the young man asked. In his twenties, he wore blue jeans and a t-shirt.

"Good guess. I'm from Kansas," Shelly said. "You are from?"

"I'm Greg, from Michigan. Lila's from Wisconsin."

Lila, dressed in Indian clothes, draped her *dupatta* on the chair next to her, revealing the *salwar kameeze* beneath. "We just got here today, Lila said. "I love this hotel, don't you?"

"Yes," Shelly agreed. "I'm fortunate to live here."

"You live *here*!" Lila said. "Do you mean Kalimpong? Or this hotel?"

Shelly laughed. "Both. I am volunteering at a veterinarian clinic, and I get room and board for taking care of the owner's dogs."

"Those Pekingese?" Greg asked. "They're always growling?"

She laughed again. "Yes, they are very naughty dogs. Where have you traveled?"

"We started six months ago," Greg said. "Where to begin!"

"Nice trip!" Shelly said. *Six months,* she agonized. *It was the equivalent of twelve years of two-weeks-with-Mark trips.* "What was your favorite?"

The young man looked at his companion, who returned an identical expression: wonderment. "Not possible. There's so much here."

"If you want the usual," Lila offered, "you go to Ajanta or the Taj."

"Yeah," he agreed. "But, if you've got the time..." Greg tore a hunk of chapatti off and dipped it in his dahl. "Well, my favorite was Bhimbetka. There're seven-hundred caves in this Teak forest, cave paintings dating back fifteen thousand years."

"Really," Shelly said. "I've never heard of it."

"No one has," he said. "We saw five people. Only fifteen of the caves are excavated now, but it's going to be amazing."

The night passed quickly talking with the new guests. The pair shared the same enthusiasm for their adventures. The old longing that she never quite had words to voice struck Shelly. She had made a deal with Mark that if she could take this volunteer position for six months, she'd marry him when she got back and they could run the pet hospital together. *Maybe he'll change his mind. I know he will if I can just get him to come once.*

On the way back to her room, she reveled in the breeze that dispersed the steamy air of the Monsoons. Once in her room, she turned off the air conditioner, threw open the windows and dressed for bed. The curtains flapped as she sat in the dark looking out on the lights of the city below. Her restlessness grew the longer she stayed in India, but a deal was a deal and she couldn't let Mark down.

Shelly fumbled in the bed stand for her cell phone and pressed the send button. Their usual time to talk was midnight for her, noon for him. "Mark?" she asked.

"Hi honey," he said.

"What are you doing?" she asked.

"Well, there're six people in the waiting room," he said. "Four dogs and a couple of cats. I need you!"

"I think of you all the time." Shelly wrapped her finger in her hair.

"What're *you* doing?" he asked.

"There's a breeze tonight, so I opened the windows. I'm watching the lights below. I wish you were here." When she heard no answer, she gripped the phone. *It's bad enough we're having trouble without the phone going out too.* "Mark? Are you still there?"

"Yes, I'm here," he said. "Sounds romantic. Anyone there with you?"

Shelly detected sarcasm. "Mark!" She stood, picked up the phone and paced. "Low blow. Please, stop."

"Sorry, Shell," he said. He expelled a long sigh. "I thought about it."

"You promised," she said. "Two weeks every year, anywhere I want to go."

"I will," he said, "but don't be unreasonable. Shell, the clinic is a success. I need you here."

"Then, when?" Her voice quavered. "What if I don't come back right away?" The phone signal faded, and then filled with static. "Mark? Mark?"

"What?" he asked. "What are you saying?"

The signal cleared and Shelly, too afraid to repeat herself, answered, "I want to see more of India. Will you come with me?"

"So... you'll take two more weeks?" he asked.

He *had* heard her and there was no turning back; she cradled the phone in both hands as if praying. "No, Mark," she said. "If you don't come, I'll be back in two months, or three or six. What does it matter?"

"Shell," he said, "what are you doing to me?"

"Nothing," she snapped, "nothing, nothing! All I'm asking is that you spend some time with me. If you can't, then what have we got? A pet clinic? A harnessed team 'til death do us part?"

"Is that what you think?" he said.

Shelly paused, sat on the back of the chair and slid into the seat. *Now I've done it,* she thought.

"Shelly? You there?"

"Yes, still here."

"You know I love you; please come home."

"Then, take the time," she said.

"You're so, so militant! This isn't like you."

"Let's talk more anther time," she said wearily.

"You're just going to leave me with an ultimatum?"

Mercifully, the phone began to fade again. After several attempts at talking above the static, she managed to tell him, "We need to talk tomorrow. I love you." Mark signed off.

He's not coming, she thought. *Where does that leave me? I compromise my life away for him. I can't bear to leave him. We're right for each other! Who am I?* She dropped her robe on the floor and crept into bed, hugging the pillow close to her chest.

****

Late that night, Shelly woke again. The dogs began to howl, not just one dog or even four dogs. Hundreds of dogs in Kalimpong, every stray, every pet—*was that Shiva? Was that Yak?* – every dog began to howl. The city straddled the saddle of a mountain pass, with a farming valley spread between it and the next populated ridge. Shelly heard dogs from both ridges, all the way up the peak above her and down to the pass below. She heard high pitches and low pitches, yips, yaps, barks, howls, bays, whines and growls. Each dog had a song of its own, and she could distinguish each one, near and far. Somewhere between one and two o'clock, it occurred to her that she was responsible to the forty thousand residents of Kalimpong for this. Through her work, these dogs survived.

In the next hour—when they did not let up or tire out—she began to hear what they said. *Do you remember what life used to be like? Yeah, all I do is sleep anymore! What happened to us? Where are my puppies? Didn't I used to nurse? I never had a summer without puppies! Where are my balls? I won that fight! Why are you still hanging around? Why is he still hanging around? Didn't we used to get it on? What happened to joy?*

By four o'clock, she understood that through her work, these street dogs would die out altogether. There would be rats. Shelly didn't sleep until the last dog whimpered to sleep near dawn.

****

Anil finished sweeping up the hair Shelly had shaved from the last dog she had spayed. "The last one today," he said.

"Good." Shelly removed her gown, walking to the row of cages. Yak was still unconscious from the morning's operation and Lakshmi slept curled around the stitches in her abdomen. "After you get Kali in a cage, take a break."

Anil set down the broom. "Got it," he said.

"We can collect more dogs after lunch."

He paused at the operating table, stroking Kali's ears. "Don't you go back to America next week?"

Shelly looked at him thoughtfully and said, "I don't know." Then she offered sarcastically, "Maybe I'll volunteer at a breeding program next."

"You cannot let the dogs bother you," he said. "You name them and get too attached."

Shelly threw her surgery coat in the laundry bin. "I can't decide. I'll be at lunch." She headed for the Fresh Bite restaurant, thinking that little bit of home might smooth the edginess she suffered from sleep deprivation.

At the door to the Fresh Bite restaurant, she stooped to pat Diva on the head and slipped the stray female a stale chapatti from the stash she always carried in her shoulder bag. Diva always slept near the newsstand next door to the restaurant, sharing her space with her two grown puppies. Without rising, Diva thumped her tail enthusiastically, capturing the chapatti between her paws, cocking her head and one notched ear to eat it.

Shelly climbed the narrow, steep stairs to the second floor. It was quiet, so she knew that school was still in session. After school, the teens—boys and girls, too—changed their prim British school uniforms for blue jeans, t-shirts and baseball caps. Free until they came of age, they spent their afternoons in a fantasy world, drinking Cokes, listening to American music and smoking. Today, after another sleepless night, Shelly felt disoriented and needed the lift her private little America would provide.

"Good afternoon, Doctor Shelly," the owner sang out. The young portly man with shining black hair grinned. "You do not come for so long time."

"*Much* too long!" Shelly followed the bustling man down the narrow aisle to the best seat in the cafe. The corner table—situated at an open-shuttered window that looked down on the narrow main shopping street—was directly between the stereo speakers.

"Doctor Shelly, I have a special CD just for you."

"Special, for me?" she said.

He wagged his head, excited. "You will have hamburger today? Same?"

"Same, same," she said.   But Indian Chai this time."

"Yes, I have," he said. "You wait now." He disappeared into the next room.

Shelly played with the yellow torn menu he had left on the table, but abruptly put it down. A brand new song blasted from the speakers. He was right. It was just for her. She heard, *Who let the dogs out? WHO—WHO who—who WHO?! Who let the dogs out?* She began to feel silly and sad all at once. *She* let them out. She most certainly *had* let the dogs out. She struggled to keep the tears that threatened to spill from her eyes hidden from the owner, who beamed from his entertainment corner. Sharp pangs of remorse for the phone conversation the night before would not let go. *Did Mark know?* She ached—heart, stomach, and limb—with the consequence of her choice. The dogs ran pell-mell down the new road stretching boundlessly.

15.
DOGS OF ECUADOR
SARAH Z. SLEEPER

Not like the cowering shadows that slink
in the alleys of L.A.
Not like the limping skeletons that die
on the sidewalks of Tijuana.
Not like the trashpile puppies of Turkey or
the chained miseries of Okinawa.

The dogs of Ecuador sleep in doorways and driveways of houses
and shops
unconcerned with feet or wheels or when
their next meal will arrive, because
it will, apparently.

"Poor people don't starve in Ecuador,"
said the guide, and neither do poor dogs.
The land is fruitful with berries, pigs and corn
sold on every corner and cart and shoulder-slung box.

They aren't afraid of people and don't need approval,
or mercy, as if the world was designed for dogs to be on their own.
As if their standard operating procedure is to walk right by and act
as if we aren't there, with them, on the street. One cat sleeps on a
round, furry dog mound, warm against the wet concrete. One man
cuddled a lucky brown pup and kissed its head again and again.

When I tried to feed the tall blonde dog in the cathedral plaza,
shoeshine men looked on and laughed.
"His name is Julio," said a half-blind cocoa vendor.
Julio wouldn't eat the potato chips I put down for him, but came to
me slowly, and I petted his filthy head. "Julio," the man called, but

Julio walked away, across the cobblestone square.

"Lady, crispas?" a filthy man said, reaching to take the bag from my hands, shoveling them down, saying something else that I couldn't understand.

I forgot his face, but I remember his filth. And I remember too, the ribs of the yellow dog, the one in Otavalo who ran past in the noon rain, with its tail between its legs.

16.
FETCH
ALISA NORRIS

The ability to hear things humans can't is one of the best parts about being a dog; even for a small one such as me. Immediately I stopped all movement as my ears perked up at a sound behind me. The sound was the *chattering* of a squirrel doing a circus act on a wire, high above the backyard. All thoughts became singular when an acorn hoarder entered the backyard. I took off running, letting out warning barks. It kept on scampering along the wire, which was smart of it. I'm ferocious.

"Reese, get back here. The squirrel's gone."

On the way back to my shady spot on the patio, my senses picked up a smell. I stopped in my tracks and made a bee-line for the funk. I breathed in and was rewarded with a stink so good. Dropping down, I rolled onto my back, making sure I was well covered in the stench.

"What are you into, now?" my owner asked.

Busted. I slinked back to the patio.

Sitting down beside my master seemed like a safe bet. I had had no intention of moving until he asked if I wanted to play fetch. He lobbed a fuzzy round object through the air which landed on the green fluffy near the tall fruit bearing giant. I jogged over to the object, which my master called a ball. The only reason I ran was because he liked this. As I approached with caution, it occurred to me that the best course of action was to sniff it. It smelled fantastic and tasted like a Milkbone dipped in bacon grease. *Yum.* This is curiously what I had for breakfast. Wait. Had he thrown the ball before? As I squeezed the ball between my jaws, I looked up to see him waving his hands in a fanning motion. Was he hot too?

"Come here! That's it."

I loped towards him with the ball clenched between my teeth. I was thirsty so I dropped the ball when my bowl had come into view.

My boss threw his hands up and said I was dumber than a box of rocks. But rocks are just rocks, they don't move. Wait... rocks? I love rocks. Where can I find a rock?

Looking from side to side, there were no rocks in sight. Then I saw my bowl and remembered I was thirsty. The clear liquid often referred to as water, felt warm on my tongue as I lapped it up. My paws were hot so I stuck one into the bowl, just to test, then the other. My master laughed which encouraged me. Splashing the entire contents out onto the patio was loads of fun.

"Fetch" was not.

Splashing was infinitely better.

A breeze caught the lock of hair which flopped over my eyes and blew it up off my face. Wind can be scary. I ran to my human for shelter. I sat at his feet enjoying his hand as it stroked my hair. After my massage, he finally stood up and got the ball. He presented it to me, so I sniffed it. It smelled like bacon.

"Okay buddy, let's do this."

Buddy was not my name, but I let it slide. He chucked the ball. *Not this again.* I'm a dog so I can't roll my eyes, but I wanted to.

Suddenly the screen door slid open. At last, a human with some sense appeared in the doorway. This might have been my only chance to get indoors, where it's cool. I dashed through the opening bringing my hind legs up underneath me as I scooted over the threshold. My master can't catch me like this. Another advantage of being a dog, is I'm quicker.

Ah! After getting another drink of water, cool this time, I laid on the kitchen floor. I actually preferred the bathroom tile, but it was too far away for now.

Sometime later, I didn't know how much later since I'm a dog; I heard my owner and his human female having a conversation. I knew they were talking about earlier because the words ball, fetch, and rock were mentioned. Then the female told my master maybe I wasn't smart enough to play fetch. *Incredible.*

The next evening (at least I thought it was), I had an idea. My master's female was staring at an unfurled newspaper. I ambled over and barked using my "outside" voice.

"You have to go outside?"

Bark... bark.

I hurried to the large clear portal to the outdoors and flung myself repeatedly against it until she opened it. I knew what I had to do and rushed outside.

She sat down in a patio chair so I could bring her a ball. She was smart like that. The ball hurled through the air as I chased after it. When it landed, I barked some more, then looked over at her. But she didn't move. How could these humans not understand what to do? What's that smell? I trotted back over to her and barked again. This was getting ridiculous.

"What?" she shook her hands at me, "what do you want?"

I ran back over to the ball and tried to look my cutest, which was difficult on account of how fierce I am.

"It's a good thing you're so adorable," she smiled.

Yap!

I ran back to her barking. She sighed then got up to fetch the ball. I wagged my tail and jumped up and down as she brought it over.

"You want this?" she asked.

Yap! Yap!

She bent down and offered the ball to me. Dumping it at her feet, I sat down and waited.

17.
FINDING JAKE
EILEEN VAN HOOK

Two years had passed since my beloved dog, Duffy, had died. It was time to find another best friend.

I called Ramapo Bergen Animal Shelter in Oakland, New Jersey, looking for a wire-haired terrier mix. That was Duffy's breed. He was a great dog and he didn't shed. I was told that they had a terrier mix in residence and they were pretty sure he didn't shed.

I took the forty-minute drive to the shelter to meet this dog called "Tucker." He was around two, medium sized, tri-colored and looked sort of terrier-like. I took him for a walk, found a grassy spot and sat down. He climbed onto my lap and placed his furry head on my shoulder. I'm sure that the staff there trained him to do that, but it worked. Paperwork was completed and arrangements were made for a required surgery that "Tucker" did not wish to consider or discuss.

A few days later, I took the sulking dog home, changed his name to "Jake" and began a new life. He (and I) adjusted beautifully. We had a rough spot about six months in when he made note of his separation anxiety by leaving his mark on all the electronics in the house. Some days I would return from work to find a poetry book, open on the living room floor. I imagined him lounging around in a smoking jacket reading sonnets. We got through those strange times and he emerged the most affectionate, mellow, best-behaved dog I have had the pleasure of loving.

Eleven years have passed. He's getting old, slowing down. So am I. Jake is one of my life's greatest blessings. Oh, and yes he sheds.

18.
FOR JERRY
PHILIPPE SHILS

I'm under the back steps
with my dog.

He spent the day there.
It's lonely like the

time I slept in a
field across from a

house. It
was cold and the

porch
light kept me half awake.

There are leaves and dirt
but mostly there's fur.

This is where we've gone to
dream and to twitch and

to bite one another's cheeks
and smooth one another's faces.

Oily nose to dusty nose. That's
how we were.

He's been drinking and drinking
and throwing up clear

so we keep the toilet lids down
and hope

for the best or the
worst. Not the in between.

He went under the culvert once.
There had

been a flood and he
was fetching sticks. He

went into a
drain and bobbed up on the

other
side like a cork.
He snatched frisbees

out of the
air like plates off a shelf.

Bury me
under the back porch
steps with my dog.

We can be
there together next to the

cool foundation of the house.

It's a place nobody looks. It's
a place everyone finds.

FOR JERRY
PHILIPPE SHILS

19.
HIDING FROM THE DEMON
MARY ANN BACK

She tries to lure me out from under the laundry tub with rawhide chews. But I stay put. I know what is to come. Tucked into this cubby, away from the windows, I can't see the lightning. Sometimes, when the dryer is running, the room is warm, and the rumbling, tumbling white noise soothes me. But only a little.

Silly people, can't they feel the storm brewing? The pressure dropping? It's like they can't hear the thunder steamrolling everything in its path, making its way straight toward us. And there's something else these people don't hear. It's the voice of the storm.

It's a low pitched growl that hums - whispered and predatory.

"I'll find you, Max. She can't save you. No one can."

"She" is the woman who tells me I'm silly to be so afraid, the one who scratches my ears and kisses my head. She may not hear the voice of the storm, but she can sense its venom. Sometimes, when it's at its worst, she stands at the window, statue-still, staring into the eyes of the monster as if she's waiting for it to pounce. Times like tonight.

"It's just a matter of when," it whispers, to the woman and me.

The woman holds her ground though her vigilance cannot keep the thunder and lightning at bay. They ebb and flow in such a furious dance, I can no longer tell when one stops and the other begins. The sky is ablaze. The wind howls, and I am dragged to the brink of madness.

"You can't escape. Why try?" It coaxes, "Listen to my voice, Max. I'm coming for you."

I do not so much hear these words as feel them spring from inside me. A slight whimper wheezes from my throat. The woman brings me a bowl of water and I realize that I'm panting. She speaks soothing words and strokes my fur. I close my eyes and mercifully drift away to a quiet place where the only voice I hear is hers.

When I awake, the woman is telling me what I already sense, that the storm has passed, that I am safe again, for now. She means well though she is powerless to keep the monster from returning. If only she could hear its voice, she would not think me silly. She doesn't understand. And yet, in spite of her ignorance, she continues to leave space beneath the laundry tub - for the next time the demon comes to call.

20.
HOME SECURITY
NEIL DOHERTY

Burglars hereabouts rejoice,
little Cody has no voice.
My little runt's a Havanese,
and doggies quite as small as these
are hardly bigger than their fleas.

Cody cares not for her size,
and should the burglar burglarize,
her silent snarl is not for show
and, undeterred by vertigo,
may bite the bugger on the toe.

Now Zachary is long of tooth
and reminisces of his youth.
He sleeps all day upon the floors
and softly dreams with twitchy paws
in between his doggy snores.

And burglars bitten on the toe
will run as fast as they can go,
past the canine on the floor,
who'll up, and nip, and raise some gore,
then settle down and sleep some more.

HOME SECURITY
NEIL DOHERTY

21.
LEARNING FROM DOGS
DARRELL LAURANT

The perception is that we are the more evolved species, dogs merely our sidekicks—Robins to our Batman, loyal and helpful but not quite as bright. But what if it's really the other way around? I started thinking about that the other day; as I was giving one of my three dogs a belly rub.

For the question shouldn't be so much "who is smarter?" as "who is happier?" We humans, in all our evolved wisdom, spend billions of collective dollars every year on psychiatrists, counselors, self-help books and videos, religion, alcohol and drugs, all in a vain effort to feel better. Is that really smart?

Dogs don't seem to have the same angst. They don't need to find themselves, because they always know who they are.

To be sure, some have lousy lives. Maybe they're chained to a tree in a sweltering backyard all summer, or abused in other ways by their owners. Maybe they suffer in their old age from some sort of pervasive and terminal ailment. Maybe they're stuck in a pound.

Yet dogs don't stress or obsess about these things, but take what joy they can from a bad situation.

Not that dogs are perfect. The same German shepherd and collie who is a loving companion at home might get in with the wrong pack and wreak havoc. Dogs can be messy sometimes, or cantankerous. They get into the garbage and steal food off your plate.

Still, there is so much we can learn from them. Here are ten ways that dogs just might be smarter (or at least less illogical) than the people they serve, protect and love.

Dogs aren't judgmental. They don't care if you are overweight, dress badly or drive an old car. They don't worry about your politics or religious affiliation. And no matter how crappy a day you've had, or how many people you've disappointed or alienated, your dog is always glad to see you when you come home.

Dogs don't bear grudges. Your dog may growl at you, but he'll forget all about it in an hour. Think how much better the world would be if groups of us weren't still stewing about wrongs committed hundreds of years ago.

Dogs are appreciative. That's what they have tails for. If only humans could remember to thank those around them for all the favors that come our way.

Dogs are fearless in defending what they believe in, whether it's their people, their home or their bone. I once had a friend with a miniature dachshund who would jump into my lap when I came over and allow me to rub his ears. But when my friend asked me to feed her dog while she was gone, he wouldn't let me past the front door. Humans, on the other hand, often allow their supposed loyalties to vanish in the wind.

Dogs are honest. I've always liked the old joke about the man who shows up at a buddy's house for a poker game and finds that his buddy's dog is one of the players. "That's the smartest dog I've ever seen," the visitor says, astonished.

"Aw, he's not so smart," replies his buddy. "He always wags his tail when he gets a good hand."

Dogs are incapable of being devious or insincere. If they don't like someone, or what's been put in their food bowl, they'll let you know.

Dogs live in the moment. They're always glad to drop what they're doing to go for a ride or chase a ball. Those of us who lay down strict schedules and refuse to deviate from them could learn a lot from that.

Dogs delight in the little things, like scraps from dinner. We humans quickly become immune to the charm of small, everyday pleasures.

Dogs aren't a slave to time. If you're gone five minutes, they greet you on your return as if it's been five days.

Dogs can set their egos aside. If they have to perform a trick to get a treat, they're okay with that.

Dogs are not obsessed by sex. Not that I'm saying people should be as uninhibited in that regard as their pets, but dogs don't seem to feel any sense of rejection if things don't work out. And if they've been fixed, well, there's always that ball to chase or food bowl to empty.

22.
LETTER FROM THE DOG
ALEXANDRA HEEP

Dear Not-a-Dog,

Of course, I don't speak Cat, I am a dog. Why don't you learn Dog? I suppose that in the meantime a letter will have to do. Of course, I don't look like anything like you because I am a dog. A wiener dog, also known as a Dachshund, to be exact. (No, not weiner). People call us hot dogs, but I don't like that. We are not food, we are dogs. See, hoomans make those stupid hot dog costumes that they put on us to make us look like the food. They think it's fun, but I don't think that is cool.

So, my life is not easy at all. Besides being burdened with that name, I have the disadvantage of my breed: short legs. That means I can't get up on the couch or bed, like you. Nor can I get to all the yummy food in the house. Do you know what it's like to smell all that delicious foodstuff and never get any of it? You can climb! I wish you would get some of the foodstuff from the top and throw it on the floor. That's even better than raiding the garbage can. Besides, you have a bowl that is full of kibbles all the time, but I get fed only once a day. It's not fair, I say. Of course, I gobble it down in one sitting then.

Also, you don't get made wet every month like I do. Bath, they call it, to make me clean. I resent the fact that everyone thinks that I am smelly or dirty. I don't smell anything. Well, what I do smell is the scent you leave behind after having lain in my bed when I am not in it. Not cool. I wish they would immerse you in the wet stuff sometimes so you could understand what that is like.

And no, I don't make my life difficult by going outside to poop or pee. I don't even need a box like you do. The floor is just fine for me. However, for some reason that is frowned upon around here. So, it's Mom and Dad who make it difficult on me by making me go outside to do the business. At least I get a reward for that. Do you get food rewards for pooping in a box? No. Who is smarter now?

Woof,

Adrianne, the Dog

23.
MILK BONE
JOHN C. MANNONE

It still sits on the dash
of my Honda Accord
even after four years
I got the call from my wife
while I was away reading
poetry at the Mudpie.
She found him
lying sickly by the door.
I don't know why. But we all
have enemies whose poison
doesn't always smell.
It was too late for the Vet.

She placed his head on her lap
to comfort him
with soft words, gentle strokes;
my car rushing, an hour away.
But every time he heard
a car approach, he struggled
to lift his head, his ears limp,
yet listening for familiar
sounds of my car, anxious to hear
the sound of my voice, waiting
for the last milk bone biscuit
I would bring.

One day, I will take it to him.

24.
MISS HEARTS
STACY FRITZ

Dogs make life so much brighter. Those big-eyed wet-nosed pooches are like tiny suns pushing the clouds away.

The current light of my life is a mostly white Morkie (Maltese/Yorkshire Terrier) mix named Hearts. She has light brown and gray ears that fold over like Piglet from *Winnie-the-Pooh* and a tail that looks like the swirl on a Dairy Queen ice cream cone. She also has black spots sprinkled in her white fur and big brown soulful eyes.

As I pull into my drive, I see her looking out the window. She stands up and her tail wags. When I walk through the door, there she is, impatiently waiting. She jumps for pure joy at the sight of me. No matter how gray my day may feel, that little ball of energy cheers me up. While it is true that I am the one who knows how to open the treat bag, I'd like to think it is mostly about me.

I first saw Hearts when she was several hours old. My brother's dog had been the little stud for the neighboring dog. My brother, Derek, was looking at picking out a puppy from the litter. White and black furry babies with eyes closed, wiggled around in the blanket-filled box. One was white with a large black spot on her back in the shape of a heart. The family named her Hearts. Derek ended up picking a little black and brown boy. In the process of helping him pick, and subsequent visits, that little brown-eyed girl stayed on my mind.

As the puppies grew, Miss Hearts' personality got bigger. Since Rocky, my brother's pick, was not ready to leave his mommy yet, I got to play with the litter of puppies multiple times. One visit, the puppies came tumbling into the living room, Hearts tackling one of her brothers and then bouncing back up. She jumped around and barked at the others to play. If they ignored her, she would get in front of them and push them with her nose. "Hey, play with me!" she seemed to say.

Though I was not looking to get a puppy, Hearts was pushing her way into my heart. It was bad timing with my work schedule. Many reasons why I shouldn't take on a puppy popped up in my mind.

The neighbor, John, asked me if I would like to take Hearts overnight to see how she got along with my Yorkie, Snickers. I brought that little wiggling white pup in the house and sat on the floor with her. Snickers gave her a sniff. Hearts squirmed to get away from me and closer to Snickers, who gave her a good once over and stood there wagging her tail. She stood watch as I played with the puppy. Hearts followed Snickers outside and around the fenced yard under my supervision. Snickers herded her back to me. Two girls fell asleep, one by my leg and one small one on my chest. That was it. She never left. John wasn't surprised. Not a bit.

When Snickers passed, Hearts remained close but respected that I needed to say goodbye. Once I had placed my sweet girl in a box, wrapped in her blanket, I sat down on the couch. Tears in my eyes, I felt Hearts next to my leg. As I scratched the top of her head, she crawled onto my lap and licked my chin.

So Hearts is my current love. She moved in three years ago and runs the house in my absence. She guards the front yard from rogue squirrels, barking a warning from her picture window perch. She runs off wild rabbits who try to invade my backyard gardens. She watches me work on my laptop, putting her muzzle on my shoulder when she deems that I have worked long enough. When I am snacking, her paw is on my shoulder or her chin is on my chest, her eyes looking up at me. When I sing, she comes and kisses me until I stop. And when I go to sleep each night, a warm pup is snuggled up to my legs.

Each day, Hearts makes me laugh and smile. As I get ready each morning, she plays in the hallway with her favorite toy. She shakes her little stuffed pig and then flops on her back, twisting this way and that while kicking her feet in the air. I cannot help but laugh at her happy play. When I laugh, she flips back to her feet and looks at me with those soulful brown eyes and her tail swishes. I swear she's saying 'I love you, mom.'

Hearts is just one of the wonderful furry loves I have had make a place in my heart over the years. I cannot imagine my life without a dog. My house might be tidier minus the strewn dog toys. Any tissue that is set down would not become shredded on the floor. And I would be able to travel without finding a trusted sitter. But I'll take the chewed toys, shredded tissues, and favors owed for watching my furry baby. My house would not be a home without a furry little kid. Dogs provide so much more than they take.

MISS HEARTS
STACY FRITZ

25.
MUSHROOM
ELISABETH WARD

She trotted into our home asking, *What can I do for you?*

We weren't sure. We didn't know that much about dogs and hadn't planned on getting one—not for a while, anyway. But Mushroom had proved irresistible at first glance.

Just the day before, my husband and I had decided to celebrate the Northeast's first sun-scented sixty-degree day of spring by taking our son and daughter, ages three and six, for a walk through Central Park to visit a new playground. Our daughter noticed a couple sitting just outside the fence, below the *No Dogs Allowed* sign, with one well-behaved mature spaniel mix and an energetic bundle of long beige hair defined as a dog only by a pink tongue, shiny black dot of a nose, and some longer hair wagging over her back from the other end.

"Can my little girl pat your puppy?" my husband asked.

The couple exchanged a satisfied look before the man holding the puppy's leash—a three-foot length of electrical cord knotted loosely around her neck—laughed out his answer.

"She can have my puppy."

It turned out they had kept Mushroom for six months only because they could not bear to part with her. When the realization came that Mushroom was a Kid's Dog and they were not being fair to either the mother or her pup, they set out to meet a family. Our very separate paths had taken us all on a different journey to the same spot.

Our two blond children, a bit shaggy themselves with their school haircuts having grown out during the course of the winter semester, forgot about the swings, slides, dirt piles and all those other things they'd looked forward to frolicking over, around and through, and spent the afternoon running circles around the outer fence, taking turns pulling and being pulled by the twenty-pound bouncing ball of fluff on the other end of the wire.

I did not want to break our children's hearts by bringing a potentially unhealthy dog into their lives, so we made arrangements to meet far downtown at the couple's veterinarian's office the next afternoon. The puppy pranced confidently down the street on her electrical cord, one step ahead of her soon-to-be-former owner, off to a new life she could never know was coming. She greeted the children, vetted out perfectly, bounced out the door with them and jumped into the back seat of our car. For once, I tried to stop at every intersection—not my usual mode of driving in Manhattan—just for the pleasure of looking in the rearview mirror at three shaggy blond heads eagerly turning side-to-side, enjoying the view outside, as well as their view of one another.

Like a lot of other mushrooms, ours was difficult to identify. We knew the mother was part spaniel and learned her mother had been a Sheltie. That explained Mushroom's instant ability to herd the children and her eagerness to retrieve them. But her mother's owners had no idea what the father had been, other than part of a friendly pack of playful dogs on the beach.

I'm not sure how long Mushroom was part of our lives before people began stopping us on the street and telling us about their Tibetan terriers, but it was an experience that became familiar. One woman went so far as to insist we should be showing her.

"But she's a mutt."

"She has every characteristic of the breed," was the determined response.

She certainly showed herself to be adept at everything, including living in a cold, snowy climate or tearing up and down mountain trails on family vacations to the high altitudes of Wyoming. But she proved most adept at being the perfect Kid's Dog.

When our children were babies, I often noticed that dogs walking with older children would look longingly after me as I pushed a pram along Upper Manhattan streets. (Umbrella strollers were in the not-so-distant future, but we didn't know that.) It was obvious to the most casual observer—yes, even to one who had only known cats as pets—that these dogs missed the days of the confined child, ached for those days of extended walks and visits on park benches, of companionship on their terms.

Mushroom was not one of those dogs. Mushroom was one of the kids. She played what they played, wore what they wore; she searched for what they searched for, she put each one of them to bed at night and, after our before-bedtime walk with her, she'd take her night biscuit and hide it under a child's pillow before curling up at the foot of our bed to see the masters through to dawn.

We also learned that, though so desperately lonely for them during the day she resembled a forgotten garment tossed beside the door, Mushroom quickly acquired a wealth of patience awaiting the moment her children would burst through that door at the end of the school day. Her joy was unbounded two months after entering our lives when she discovered summer vacations in the country.

We spent these days lakeside at our large extended family's small beach, or on horseback in the fields, or picking vegetables in the family's garden. The beach was below a bluff, reachable by a steep, windy road that dropped from the half-mile long driveway snaking along a hillside from the main road. A footpath through the woods, far enough below the drive to remain unseen, connected our houses to the beach. Unless we were on our way to town or on our bikes—or in a big hurry—we usually used the footpath. Mushroom knew each spot well for, of course, she tagged along.

She enjoyed swimming and presented a vision of buoyancy, guard hairs drifting about her like a furry jellyfish, until they became waterlogged and she rode lower and lower in the water, at which point she'd head for shore.

She rode on my lap in my kayak while a child straddled bow and stern or sat in the rowboat while we fished. Her boat manners were superb. She did dive once from shore when our son, then age five burst into tears as his trout flipped and tossed the hook. No matter how wet her guard hairs, Mushroom never lost enough buoyancy to retrieve that fish.

When our children were old enough to venture out alone on their sailboards, Mushroom accompanied me in the family's Boston Whaler on those days they were becalmed and required a tow home. The Whaler was moored in our dock's second slip. The rowboat was tied in the first slip. Mushroom knew the sound our feet made against each boat, so was ready to come running to leap in before an engine caught or oar met oarlock.

Pets never live long enough. This is not the beginning of a sad story—unless you're Mushroom and want to live in Never Never Land where children don't grow up. Mushroom lived long enough to see her children go away to college. For a dog on which every hair drooped when her kids walked down the street to school, taking them by car and leaving them at a distant array of buildings we called a *campus* was the next thing to a death sentence. We moved permanently to the country where she could spend her days alongside my horse in open fields or behind me on cross-country ski trails instead of listening for familiar voices from the street. But it wasn't the same, and we both knew that not-too-deep inside we both longed for June and dreaded September.

We were told Tibetan Terriers are known for longevity, and Mushroom seemed bent on proving it. Still, she had other blood and, though carrying on her puppy ways, Mushroom slowly lost first her vision, then her hearing. But she never lost her place. Perhaps all that hair in front of her eyes made her sense of smell more important. We know her guard hairs, which we referred to as her buffer hairs during rough-and-tumble moments, served as feelers. Perhaps her herding instinct mapped out a course in her brain that resembled a GPS (something else that hadn't been invented yet—except maybe by a Tibetan terrier). Perhaps her need to serve her family provided other instincts nobody may ever discover. Whatever, Mushroom remained a full member of the family, included in almost every event.

I should have made clear earlier that when I talk about our family's outdoor activities, I'm usually referring to the four of us—boy, girl, dog, mother—and sometimes cousins or our children's friends. My husband is more of an organized sports type and did not enjoy swimming, fishing, riding or cross-country skiing, but he did enjoy buzzing about the lake in the Boston Whaler.

Sometime in the middle of Mushroom's fourteenth summer... Allow me to set the scene:

Son paddling across the lake in a makeshift canoe, daughter and mother on sailboards some thirty-feet off the end of the dock trying to pick up any kind of wind, dog lying on her stomach on the beach letting the breeze play against her many guard hairs. Father walks down the wooded path, having decided to take the Whaler for a spin. He looks around, sees everyone happily engaged in activities, walks onto the dock, steps into the Whaler, starts the engine.

"NO!" my daughter and I screamed, for we knew Mushroom, blind and deaf or not, knew our habits. She felt the engine's rumble, raised her patent-leather nose in search of proof we were headed into the lake. Across the sand she flew, furry feet telling her she was on the dock, at the slip, airborne, and...

Our son heard our shout and headed back, sizing up the situation as he paddled. My daughter and I swung our rudders frantically in attempts to gain some momentum. My husband, too late, understood our cry and cut the engine.

Everyone but Mushroom heard her splash.

The dog was hidden from our view by the dock, and from my husband's view by the boat. He leapt into the water to rescue our beloved pet, thereby losing the pair of glasses required to find her. Our daughter and I watched helplessly as he flailed the water in search of his glasses. Our son went after the drifting boat.

Our helplessness was not out of concern for Mushroom, for by now we were able to see her standing on the shore shaking off enough water to be once again wetted by the miniature rainstorm she created. We were too far away from the others to be able to inform them that the dog had done the logical thing: swum to shore, where she sat patiently awaiting the boat's return.

One summer evening, not long before our lengthy northern twilight crept up, I had to run home to make a telephone call. (What! Cell phones hadn't been invented then either?!) The kids were busy toting their sailboards up the beach, tying up the sails and preparing the beach for the night. Mushroom, of course, was waiting for everyone to finish and go home.

We're not sure when she realized Mom the Boss had left the premises because neither son nor daughter saw Mushroom leave. I met her running full tilt up the beach path, hair blowing away from her face, tail drifting out behind her. Overjoyed to find me, she once again became the flying fluffball of her youth, running circles around me. Before we could reach the beach, our daughter heard and came running down from the drive.

"Oh, thank goodness! We saw her disappear toward the barn, so I went there and my brother went to the garden. We must have just missed her both places."

Somehow while the sailors were packing it in for the day, Mushroom had navigated all her landmarks in search of me.

Toward the end of her fifteenth year, Mushroom's youthful heart began to slow. She suffered her first fainting spell racing our son up the beach path. He burst into the house, Mushroom in his arms. "Mushy collapsed! She was running, and she just collapsed. She seems okay now."

Indeed, when he put her down, she jumped happily about. That event remained an isolated incident for the remainder of the summer but come fall, after the kids returned to school, I noticed she became woozy if she stood up quickly. It seemed she could exert when active but not suddenly.

"We have medication for that," our vet told me.

My husband and I talked it out for weeks, all the while watching our perennial puppy bound eagerly about—so long as she did not move suddenly. We decided to forego the medication and be careful about not startling her. There was something "invalid-y" about the idea of her going on a heart medication, and we didn't like the idea of "keeping her alive" so she could go slowly downhill.

"If she jumps up to greet me one day and dies, so be it. How many animals can die so happy?" I asked. No one argued. Not my husband, not the vet, not even our children because they knew Mushroom wanted to live on her terms.

The week our extended family gathered for my husband's mother's funeral, Mushroom was ecstatic. Here it was, School Time, and everyone was home. Our little dog was kept as busy as a puppy greeting people and counting feet.

But, inevitably, I returned to an empty house unannounced. Mushroom jumped up to greet me and died... Or didn't.

I grabbed her, wrapped my mouth around her shaggy little snout and began puffing breath into her. My husband walked in during the first round: fifteen quick breaths five times in succession followed by a "Puppy lick my face."

I was on the third round when he noticed the mess in my lap, the natural expulsion of a dying body.

"It's no use," he said. "I can't believe this happened now."

But she was still warm, so I kept puffing. Another fifteen quick breaths five times, another, "Puppy lick my face." Then another... And another.

Then, a pale tongue more white than pink touched my nose.

I kept puffing. The tongue came out again. Then again, not quite so pale. Then her eyes opened. Yes, her hairs had separated enough that my husband saw them.

"She's back!"

My husband said later it looked like I was eating my words. "Just going to let her jump up and die happy, huh."

Well, the timing just wasn't right. When would it be right, we wondered? Should we start those meds? I was perfectly willing to offer my exhalations for her inhalations again—yes, despite her old-dog breath. And during the year if I saw her knees wobble I would pick her up, give a gentle round or two, and she'd walk away on steady feet.

A year later we all convened for a family wedding. Our children came home from school and Mushroom was once again in the middle of things. But, we knew after the weekend it would be several months before they returned home. As they said their tearful goodbyes to their puppy, we hoped everyone but Mushroom knew those goodbyes would be permanent. It was time to let Mushroom drift away. And drift away she did. One night she jumped up to greet our cat as it came in through the pet door, then she collapsed in my lap.

Mushroom did live long enough, by her standards anyway if not by ours. She had done what she could for us: raised our children, protected us, even raised the cat she'd found as a kitten on the street. She couldn't do anything else but make us cry over her. And that was something she shouldn't live to see.

26.
MY CANINE FRIEND
CELIA P. RANSOM

She cocked her head and looked at me
With intelligent eyes, this magnificent Welsh Corgi.
She knew, I swear, that I was sad
For that day lay dead, my dad.
My heart was breaking o'er such tremendous loss
But she settled next to me and with her paws
Touched my arm in a comforting gesture
A simple canine moment that helped lift the pain, the pressure.
And as I stroked her coat again and again
She was what I needed—a quiet but sympathetic friend.

27.
MY DOG SNORES
A.J. HUFFMAN

when he sleeps on his back,
body stretched to fit full
length of bed. A gentle nudge
to butt or shake of hand on chest
to stop elicits a series of stuttering
snorts that sound more like a human
suffering from severe case
of post nasal drip.

28.
MY DOG WAS A HOT DOG
A.J. HUFFMAN

for Halloween this year. Not exactly
ironic, I know, but his tail
twitching at the end
of an overstuffed puff
of would-be food was too hysterical
to resist. He remained reticent,
resigned to this latest fate, laid on the same
spot of couch for hours. I imagined
I could see steam rising
from his frustrated mind. I wanted to feel
bad, but the vision only made me laugh.
I patted his tolerant head,
pulled two of his favorite treats from the drawer,
promised him next year
he could pick his own costume.

29.
MY FATHER'S DOGS
ELIZABETH MCMUNN-TETANGCO

My father dreamed
of dogs:

coils of teeth
and narrow eyes.

He fought them
in his sleep
beneath antique
chandeliers

and hotel ceilings.

He told me I was safe

but he would not say
their names.

First appeared in Hobard, November 12, 2014

30.
MY MACK MAN
NICOLE KOPPIN

Anyone who has truly loved an animal knows that a pet is much more than just a dog or cat living in your home, eating your food, and sleeping on your furniture. They become a huge part of your life! They steal a part of your heart in a way nothing else could. A pet is much more than a guardian or a companion. They become family and as part of the family you would do anything for them; enter my Mack Man.

I adopted Mack rather recently, in June 2014. I went to the Animal Welfare Society in Madison Heights, Michigan looking for a guard dog and companion for my other dog Vixen. She would bark at strangers but as a single female at the time I was concerned for my safety and decided to adopt my protector. Mack was the only dog at the shelter that didn't hide at the back of the kennel or rush the gate when I walked in. He was interesting in appearance, they had him labeled as an Australian Shepherd/Lab mix, but from my perspective I saw Rottweiler in his face. He walked to the gate of his kennel, lifted a single paw at me, and wagged his tail. That was it, I was his!

I filled out the paperwork for adoption, was approved and able to pick him up the next day. The Veterinarian determined he was not an Australian Shepherd/Lab mix and was actually a Pit Bull/Beagle mix, you can imagine the depth of a Pit Bull bark mixed with a beagle howl; quite interesting for sure! He was very well behaved and got along with Vixen and my two cats almost instantly.

Mack took a part of my heart that no other animal had before him. He became my baby. He was at my side the second I felt the slightest tinge of sorrow. He was always at my feet when I was reading or watching TV. At night, he would sleep in my bed with his head on my knees or ankles.   When we would go for walks, he was always on guard. Observant and protective, acknowledging any strange noise or object without being aggressive. His tail was always wagging; he is just the happiest dog! He's a clown as well, running into walls and tripping over his own big paws.

One night in November the pups and I went to bed as usual. Mack slept pressed against my back and I was facing the window. My alarm went off at five-thirty in the morning to get ready for work, I decided to hit snooze and get five more minutes of sleep. Mack stood up shook his head, fell off the bed and began convulsing on the floor. I jumped out of bed and pulled him away from the night stand where he was repeatedly hitting his head, and tried to steady his head. When Mack's seizure was over, he looked at me with such terror and didn't even seem to know who I was. A piece of my heart felt like it had been ripped out. My poor little boy laid there on the ground for three minutes before trying to get up; I sat there petting him telling him it would be alright. After what felt like hours later he got up and wanted to go outside. I sobbed on the phone to the emergency vet and they said there was nothing anyone could do unless another seizure occurred.

Two weeks went by without incident; I had hoped it was a fluke. It was a Saturday morning. I had woken up to hear what sounded like dog tags jingling. I ran into the kitchen and saw Mack was having another seizure. I rushed him into the vet where he had yet again another seizure. Blood was drawn for testing and medication was prescribed to help manage his seizures. I anxiously awaited the results from the blood work, hoping there would be some magical answer that would stop his seizures. When I got the call from the vet my prayers were unanswered, everything was normal.

I was devastated. Normal wasn't having to worry about sleeping because Mack might have a seizure in the middle of the night. Normal wasn't worrying about my other pets, my boyfriend

Alex, or myself because Mack had shown aggression while coming out of a seizure before. Normal isn't being helpless while I watch my sweet, loving boy convulse on the floor and know there is nothing I can do to help him. None of this was normal!

A few more weeks and a few more normal blood tests later we had our worst night yet. My boyfriend and I woke up at two-thirty in the morning to the sound of Mack seizing on the kitchen floor. We raced to the kitchen getting the other pets safely out of the area. When Mack came out of it he was racing around the house, blind for longer than usual, running into everything. I sat on the couch next to Alex and cried. That's when I noticed there was urine on the carpet; Mack had a seizure in the living room previous to the one in the kitchen.

While Alex and I were trying to comfort each other and the dog, Mack collapsed in the living room by the front door and had a third seizure in a ten minute time frame. I was beyond devastated. I knew multiple seizures could destroy brain cells and I was concerned we would have to put my baby down if the seizures didn't stop. I called the emergency vet and they said all they could do is monitor him. We waited until my vet opened watching him carefully and listening for any signs of seizure activity. They put him on another medication to help manage his seizures and drew more blood for testing.

Since that night, he has had two minor seizures that we are aware of. His activity level is more normal. He's back to his wiggly, loving, clumsy self! The medication has done wonders. I know it won't always be rainbows and butterflies, and every time he has a seizure it rips a piece of my heart knowing there is nothing I can do to help him. Despite all the upsets, he is still my baby. Mack still holds a special place in my heart and I will do whatever is necessary to keep him healthy and happy for however long or short his life may be.

A pet truly does become a part of the family. There may be struggles and hardships along the way, but there is something about that goofy grin, silly howl, and the way he trips over his own paws that makes it all worth it!

MY MACK MAN
NICHOLE KOPPIN

31.
PAWS TO READ
PATRICIA HOLLAND

The big white dog looked as eager as the old man on the other end of the leash. As they entered the school library, the dog's tail began a metronome wag when he saw three of his furry friends already in their down-stay position. Or maybe he was wagging because he spotted a little boy clutching a book and nervously waiting to start his Paws-to-Read session.

The portly old man looked a lot like Santa Claus. He smiled as he spoke to the skinny little boy. "Hello again, I remember you from one of our fall reading sessions. My name is Al Harrison and this is my dog Polar Bear—Bear for short. We love reading. Where've you been? We've missed reading with you."

"My name is Tad. My new daddy made me sign up this spring." *Humm, there must be quite a story there.* The boy had a new scar, a reddened, jagged scar that ran from his hairline down past a drooping eyelid to his upper lip. *I bet that's a dog bite*, Al thought.

He remembered the boy from their reading sessions last year. The librarian said the eight-year-old boy had low self-esteem and was developing a stutter whenever he read aloud. Tad was a transfer and way behind in his classes. She hoped reading to a dog would give him more confidence. Al put Bear into a down-stay, right next to a big pillow. That pillow wasn't for the dog, it was for the child. Al patted the pillow and asked the boy to sit down. "You know how much Bear likes books. He'll listen while you read aloud."

Tad dutifully read the first pages to the dog, slowly pausing when he stuttered or stumbled over unfamiliar words. Then as he read page after page to Bear, his stuttering stopped.

At the end of the chapter, he closed his book and reached over to pet Bear. Tad wanted to talk to Bear and to Mr. Harrison. "My mom's boyfriend came to live with us just before Christmas. I'm supposed to call him daddy, but they aren't married. He has a big dog that doesn't like me." Tad described the day the dog bit him. "I walked home after school. When I opened the front gate and the dog ran up to me. I was just going to pet him. But when I looked at him he started growling and knocked me over. Then he bit me. I had twenty-two stitches, right here" he said as he pointed to his face.

Some gently probing questions from Al followed. He learned that the boyfriend, Tad called "daddy," was up against an ultimatum from Tad's mom. The man could not bring his dog back into her home until Tad would be okay with it.

At the end of the reading period, Al told the boy, "Bear and I enjoyed listening to you read today. I hope you'll come back for the Paws-to-Read session next week." He went on, "It's a beautiful spring day. After I leave the library, I'm going run a few errands then I'll take Bear across the street to the dog park. We'll be there for a while. After school, see if you can get your new daddy to walk over to the park with you. I'd like to talk to him."

****

The big sign at the gate read "Dog Park." It was a special place, with several grassy acres safely enclosed in a boundary fence. It was a haven and heaven for dogs.

As Al Harrison brought Bear in through the park gate, he detoured around a tattooed man with his unruly big dog and his little boy. Tad had persuaded his new dad to come to the park, but Al had not expected "Daddy" to bring along his dog.

The boy looked scared. His face was marred by the jagged scar that ran from his hairline, down past a drooping eyelid to his upper lip. Al knew there were inner scars to go with Tad's visible one. It looked like Tad was afraid of both the man and his dog. Al eavesdropped on their conversation.

"Here you go Tad, you just need to get used to being around dogs. Enjoy yourself. Go play" the man said. The man gave Tad a shove, "We're going to stay here for an hour or so to get you used to dogs. Go on we're not leaving until you pet a dog."

Al let Bear off leash and started to walk in the direction of his favorite bench. But his big, white dog stood stock still because the little boy had backed into him.

The old man turned around and smiled at the boy. He winked as he said, "Hello again, remember me? My name is Al Harrison and this is my dog Polar Bear—Bear for short. You read your book to him in the library today. I'm sure he'd like you to pet him, and he won't hurt you."

Tad looked up. "My daddy pushed me into your dog. I'm sorry."

"The kid says he's afraid of dogs. He needs to get over it" the man said as he stuck out his hand for a shake. "My name is Butch Goodwin. Tad has just been telling me about reading to Bear. He told me Bear was as big as a sofa."

"Well now," the old man looked at the tattoo-covered fellow. "Bear likes Tad and I think Tad likes Bear. I'm going over there to sit on that bench. Why don't you both walk over there with me?" Goodwin and the boy readily complied and trailed along after the old man, but he kept his distance from his new daddy's dog.

"I'm not afraid of every dog. I like your dog," Tad said. "It's just other dogs, like the one that bit me." He pointed to the young, muscular black and tan dog Butch had let it off its leash.

If I didn't already have grey hair deciding whether or not to put my oar into this mess would make me go grey, Al Harrison thought. He said, "I think the biggest mistake you can make after a child becomes afraid of dogs is to discount his fear and assume he can forgive and forget what happened. You should let the child set the pace, let him say when he's ready to go closer to that dog."

Al settled down on the bench. "Now watch what Bear does for the next few minutes. First Bear needs to find a tree. Then he'll play with his dog friends. When he gets tired, he'll come back over here to his people friends."

The warm air and flowering signs of spring brought many families to the Dog Park. As soon as they walked into the park, most of the people took their dogs off their leashes. Some of the dogs immediately took off, running in joyous circles. Some male dogs, like Bear, marched from tree to tree leaving a few drops of urine on each one—leaving doggy calling cards. Some dogs sniffed at other dogs in a friendly way.

Al told Tad, "Bear might bring some of his friends back with him so let's talk about what to do if a dog you don't know walks up to you. If the dog is with its owner, always ask if you can pet it before you go any closer. The owner should know whether or not the dog is friendly." Al glanced at the boy' stepdad, who looked a bit worried.

"Dogs can't speak so they say hello by using their noses to sniff. Sit still. Just keep looking at me, don't bend over and stare into the face any dogs you don't know. That may seem threatening to them" Al told Tad.

"Dogs first check you out by sniffing you. The dog that just sniffed Bear is another Paws-to-Read dog. I know him. He's very friendly. He's probably going to sniff you next and he might give you a kiss! Ah, yes. You've just had a doggie kiss. Tad, that quick smooch was the dog's way of giving you the okay, a doggie way of getting to know you better."

Now if I can figure out how to get a few minutes alone with Tad's stepdad to get to know him better I might be able to help them both, Al thought. "Tad, I'm going to put Bear's leash on again, so you can practice walking together. He's trained to heel. So whenever you say 'heel,' he'll walk beside you on your left side. Hold the leash and step out as you say 'heel.'"

After Tad and Bear walked away, Al turned to Tad's new daddy. "We need to talk. I think you're pushing Tad too hard to overcome his fear of your dog. He wants you to like him, but it can't be easy for him to get over a dog bite that left him with that big scar running down his face."

"I've a problem right now. I love Tad's mom and I love that kid, but I love my dog, Fang, too. The pup never attacked anybody before. Now Tad's mom won't let my dog back in the house until the kid overcomes his fear. My brother is keeping my dog chained up in his backyard. That's no way to treat a dog. It's not a good place for Fang."

"I agree with you about chaining up the dog, Mr. Goodwin. Tell me the truth. Did you train that dog to attack strangers?"

"When I lived at my brother's place we depended on his old dog to protect the stuff we had in the yard and stuff we kept in the house. I never taught Fang anything, but he might have learned to bark and lunge at strangers from watching how the old dog treated people who came into the yard."

"Keeping your young dog at your brother's place doesn't sound like a really good solution, but pushing Tad so hard isn't good either. Have you noticed his stutter has come back?"

"What can I do?" the man asked.

"I have a friend who trains big dogs," said Al. "She could evaluate your dog's behavior to see if it will ever be suitable as a family pet. She can also give it some obedience training. If she thinks the dog can be socialized and trained, then I could foster your dog for a month or two to get it unchained and out of your brother's yard. Let me call her right now." Al said.

****

By the time Tad and Bear came back, Butch had talked to the trainer and agreed to send Fang to her for training. Then Al gave him a home temporarily. By the end of the school year, after Al had fostered him for two months, Tad and his mom let Butch bring his dog back into their house. As his fears diminished and his scars faded, Tad gradually made friends with Butch's dog.

One day when Tad saw Mr. Harrison at the Dog Park, he said he had decided to rename Fang. "I don't like the name Fang. It reminds me that he had big teeth" Tad said. "I'm going to call him Prince from now on."

"That's a really good name. Besides, he's turning into a really good dog" Al said.

"I want to change your name too. Can I call you granddad?" Tad asked.

"I'd be honored and happy to have you call me granddad. Thank you, Tad." Al realized his devotion to his big dog and to the boy in the reading program had given him a grandson—and another dog to love.

That summer, Tad signed up his newly-named Prince for obedience classes at the dog park. Granddad Harrison decided to sign up Bear too. The dog had already had obedience training, but the old man just wanted to spend some time with his newly-adopted family.

During the first obedience class, Tad worked with Bear while Butch worked with Prince. Then, as Tad gained more confidence, he began working with Prince, who was maturing into a reliable, controllable, and best of all, trustworthy dog.

The following spring, just about a year after he met Tad, Al Harrison attended an unusual chapel wedding—dogs allowed. Butch and Tad's mom invited him to their wedding. As the organist played the Wedding March, the Best Man, Tad, proudly walked up the aisle with Prince heeling at his side. Then Granddad Al and Bear escorted the bride up the aisle. After the bride and groom exchanged their vows and kissed, they drew Tad and his Granddad Al into their arms for a group hug. The family—and their dogs— came back down the aisle together.

32.
PIGGY
RICK BLUM

He bounds up to me with a head full of vim
and a mouth full of stuffed pig. Go ahead,
he says, take it away from me tough guy;
I don't think you've got the moxie to do it.

But I'm no wuss, so I grab a delicately dangling piggy leg
and give a good yank, to no avail, of course, as he's got
piggy's head firmly locked between ten well-honed
incisors and is not about to relinquish this treasure easily.

After ten or fifteen seconds of me yanking, him
pulling and growling (just to show he means business),
I let go, which sets off several dervish-like bouts
of piggy shaking, furious enough to kill a small moose,
which was nature's original intent, after all.

But piggy never dies, only comes apart at the seams.
Tonight, though, piggy returns whole, cork-screwed
tail first, for another round of I-dare-you-to-take-it-away,
followed by more flailing and growling, then another
take-it-away challenge.

Eventually, I tire of the game, settling back into my
plumped-up chair for an evening of soporific sitcoms
and who-dun-its.

Without a foil to keep up the warrior pretense, he
gives piggy a few, last perfunctory chews to make sure
it won't come back to life, then jumps up on *his* end
of the sofa, rests a weary head on the arm and looks
at me with droopy, chocolate-drop eyes that say
life will never be this good again.

And he might be right.

PIGGY
RICK BLUM

33.
SATISFACTION DENIED
GARY BECK

A poet once said that April is the cruelest month. If so, May must be the horniest month. Another winter had gone by without any improvement in our sex life. The few girls I had dates with hadn't been interested in getting physical. I never figured out what they wanted, but it sure wasn't casual sex. My acting students at Gotham University's School of the Arts had shed their winter coats and some of the girls were revealing more and more of their tantalizing flesh. *O, lead me not into temptation.* And, as if things weren't bad enough for me, my dog Pard's sexual urges were coming back stronger than ever. This caused another incident in Tompkins Square Park. We were at the dog run for the after-work walk, when Pard spotted a Mommy's darling Pomeranian that looked like a miniature, plump red fox. Pard dashed to her for the usual under the tail inspection, recognized the appropriate orifice and tried to mount her. Even crouching down it was a physically impossible task. Nevertheless, he unsheathed his glistening, red thing, rubbed it on her luxurious fur coat and ejaculated all over her.

The Pomeranian's look-alike mistress screeched in horror, attracting the attention of other dog walkers. They gathered around her, clucking sympathetically, offering consolation after the vile desecration of her alter ego. The incident was about to blow over, when from the safety of the crowd, the same limp-dick that I had a run-in with last year in similar circumstances, yelled: "You should have that mutt fixed." Other voices murmured in support. This time I didn't make a smart ass comment. I apologized profusely and promised to keep my dog under better control. I was very reassuring and the lynch mob didn't materialize. Mr. Limp-dick kept agitating to string me up, or at least banish me, but the others lost interest. By the time Pard and I left the park, the tension had abated. However, I still had many baleful thoughts about Mr. Limp-dick. *Imagine suggesting that I cut off my best friend's balls. Ugh. What a scuz.*

So once again the urgent need for sex had reared its demanding head. I was just settling in for some serious brooding about the desperation of man and beast, when the phone rang. It was Anitra, my former girlfriend, calling from India. The artist she worked for, who I had nicknamed Sophisto, the master of plastic, was negotiating to wrap the Taj Mahal. I related my tale of woe and her response was as frigid as usual and just as intolerant. "You have to learn to control these urges and not let them dominate your life."

"That's easy for you to say. It's not your problem."

"Don't be bitter. In the past, men have sublimated their baser instincts into art and created wonderful work. You're a writer. Try to elevate yourself."

"Okay. That's my situation. What about Pard? He can't sublimate his sex drive."

"There is a traditional remedy for that." She didn't have to spell it out.

"I wouldn't do that to him," I said indignantly.

During her long silence, I wondered if there was a ballcutters lodge out there, somewhere, dedicated to the removal of male organs. Just as I was visualizing the Loyal Order of Castrators initiating novices into the mysteries of eunuchdom, Anitra interrupted my reverie. "Your dog has a diagnosable condition; too much glandular activity. Perhaps Prozac or some other pharmaceutical would alleviate the problem."

"Are you saying he's oversexed?"

"What do you call it?"

"Normal doggie behavior," I replied righteously.

"That's not how others see it."

"They can be wrong."

"Take him to your vet and ask him to prescribe something."

"I'll think about it," I muttered sullenly.

"Don't sulk. It's babyish... Now our next project will be to wrap the Empire State Building, so I'll be in New York soon."

"That's all we need," I quipped without thinking, "a gigantic condom in midtown Manhattan."

The distant silence reminded me that I couldn't keep my big mouth shut, and it was confirmed when she said glacially: "I'll call you when I get to New York."

Once again, I only had my own resources to draw on, and they were stretched to translucency. I remembered the one thing I had learned in previous crises; the worst case scenario was to feel sorry for myself and do nothing. I pondered for almost an hour how to alleviate Pard's sex needs and couldn't come up with anything new. In desperation, I jotted down everything I had tried so far, including my shameful, short-lived efforts as a doggie procurer. I picked up a copy of the "Doggie Tribune," the newsletter I published to try and find a female for Pard. I thought it had been a brilliant inspiration and I tried to assess why it had been so unsuccessful. After objective analysis, I concluded that it was clever, witty, entertaining and well written. I couldn't understand why it failed. Perhaps I didn't reach a wide enough or diversified readership. Maybe it was a circulation problem. The bitch of Pard's dreams might live in Chelsea or the upper west side, completely unaware of his existence. I succumbed to fantasy for a moment, imagining the gnomes at the New York Times ordering the destruction of my publication to stifle competition. Then it came to me in a flash; radio and TV had a much bigger audience than a humble monthly newsletter.

I began to consider radio talk shows and call-in programs and made a note to get a radio program guide. A little research might identify an appropriate show. TV shows were more complicated. Even if I could get on a TV show, it would at most be a comedy or late night talk show. Then everyone would just see me as a wacko who wanted to get his dog laid. That wasn't an image I looked forward to. Yet an idea was tickling the back of my brain, hinting that I was on the track of something. I thought and thought about the basic problem; how to get Pard's ashes hauled without looking like a loony, but I still couldn't come up with a solution. No talk show host would take my quest seriously and would probably subject me to ridicule. I was about to go back to the silly foibles of Restoration comedy in the plays of Aphra Behn, when inspiration struck. If I produced my own show for public access, I could control the content and present any image that I wanted. This was an exciting possibility. Now all I had to do was to find out if it was practical.

The next morning I called the Manhattan public access station and they promised to send me their producer's handbook. They weren't too responsive when I urged them to send it special delivery. The next two days passed as sluggishly as chilled molasses while I waited impatiently for the booklet to arrive. My frequent visits to the mailbox didn't help any. But the station kept their word and when I got home on the third day it was waiting for me. I tried to read it before the after-work dog walk, but Pard kept bringing me his leash and barking when I didn't respond. The call for lights, action, camera would have to wait until we got back from the park.

The usual villains who detested my dog were already in the dog run, so I took Pard to the fringes of the park. Naturally, just as Pard squatted and expunged the day's accumulation of waste, a cop saw us. He rushed at us shouting dreadful accusations and it was too late to flee. I filibustered, reasoned, flattered, cajoled and groveled to no avail. He gave me a fifty dollar ticket. "Thanks a lot, officer. He was just fertilizing the grass."

"Do you want to tell it to the judge, wiseguy?" I wagged my head no and slunk off.

I cursed impotently all the way home, while Pard, frolicked, blissfully unaware of the cost of depositing fecal matter in a public park, outside the dog run. By the time I fed Pard and sat down to read the producer's handbook, my anger had dissipated. There were pages of rules and requirements, but the meaning was clear; any citizen of the borough of Manhattan could air a program of thirty or sixty minutes on request. The facilities of the Manhattan public access station could be used to produce a program if you took their training course on their equipment. Could it be that simple? All I had to do was qualify on their equipment, then produce my show. *If it was that easy, why wasn't everyone producing their own shows?* Maybe I was being a bit paranoid, but there had to be a catch somewhere. I made a note to find out more about how the public access stations worked. I also decided to watch the public access stations. Maybe every nut and her brother were already producing programming.

Now that I knew I could make my own show, I had to figure out what it would be. Nothing would be more boring than my just talking to the audience, droning on and on about a dog's need for sex, looking like a complete lunatic, raving on the airwaves. This obviously called for a creative approach to the problem of how to make an interesting show with limited resources. That sounded familiar from my experience in theater. Since this show was for television, I needed a visual concept. I didn't have artistic skills, so I found it difficult to make exciting images. Maybe I could use pictures from books and talk without being seen on camera. Maybe photos or reproductions of paintings could be used, if that was allowed. If I could get some actors, I could write a script and direct them. Some of my students would be interested in gaining television experience... No. Definitely not. The topic of doggie sex would spread throughout the school and 'Ernest the emoter', my boss, and the head of the theater department, would pillory me. I'd have to find another way to get actors.

I tried to remember if any of the actors I had worked with Off-Off-Broadway were suitable. The only one I could think of with real talent was a scruffy lout, who had played Hamlet, set in a mental institution. He was so disheveled that he would look like a compost heap on TV. *If I had a better idea what the show was about, I would have a clearer picture of what I needed.* A talk show might be the simplest format. A host, two guests, and a basic set might be sufficient. I didn't want to appear on camera, so I had to have three actors. If the host was a trendy, upscale woman, the man and woman guest might seem legitimate. It would also disguise the underlying motive; cheap sex for Pard. It was time to outline a script to find out if the idea was really practical.

I sketched out several ideas and finally came up with what seemed like a viable format. The host would present the topics to the guests. The woman guest would oppose the use of pharmaceuticals to control dog behavior. The host could ask: 'What about the sexual urges of male dogs. They offend many people.' The guest would respond: 'They are natural occurrences and should be dealt with accordingly.' The host would continue: 'What do you suggest?' I didn't quite have the answer to that yet, but I noted that if the guest started with a humorous reply, it might relax viewers. The male guest would strenuously object to the extravagant expenditures that dog owners squandered on their privileged pets while homeless children went hungry. The host would agree with the basic premise and suggest that the pet owners who spent large amounts of money on fashionable doggie mink coats and jewelry should make contributions to charitable groups that fed the needy. The host could end the show by asking the viewers to write their reactions to the same P.O. Box that I used for the short-lived 'Doggie Tribune.'

I was very satisfied with the first outline for a script. The next step would be to write a draft and come up with a name for the show. So far, so good. The technical part of video production now had to be explored. Did I need a crew, or could I learn enough to operate the cameras myself? What about lighting, video tape, sets, and costumes? There were specific problems that had to be resolved before I placed a call for actors in the theater trade papers. There was no point in having a cast if we couldn't do the show. I had to read the producer's handbook thoroughly, prepare a list of all my production needs and make sure I asked the right questions. It seemed simple enough to direct the actors, but the technical side of video production was a mystery to me. I wondered if there was public access production information on the internet and made a note to go on-line at the library and see what I could find.

The next day I went to the library, but the results were disappointing. The chat rooms featured endless ramblings about the anguish of production from sensitive video artistes, but no meaningful technical information. I briefly considered phoning Anitra in Paris and asking her for help, but rejected that thought when I remembered her attitude towards sex. She was as intolerant of Pard's needs as she was of mine. So I signed up for the training course at the public access station and was invited to attend the following morning. It was an interesting session, albeit superficial, but I was introduced to the basics of camera, audio, directing, lighting, editing, etc. The station's staff were very helpful and patiently answered the silliest questions. The end result was my realization that to produce a show of acceptable quality I needed a crew of three, besides myself. This was completely impractical at present and I rejected the compromise of a low-grade production that would consist of only one talking head. I was back where I started from; no relief for Pard.

I had always been a bit of an obsessive/compulsive, but the situation with Pard had gone way beyond previous experiences. All my efforts on the poor mutt's behalf had come to naught. I couldn't be proud of the many different things I had tried because they had all failed ignominiously. Well, the 'Doggie Tribune' was clever, although Pulitzer ineligible. Then, just as I was relegating Pard to monasticism, the last hope came to me in a flash; the internet. Thousands, maybe millions of weirdos, ego enhancers, droners, babblers, gossips, pseudo-intellectuals, and know-it-alls filled the invisible lines with gaseous emissions that linked us together. There had to be a chat room concerned with dog problems. If not, I could easily start one. Perhaps there was still a way to help Pard.

Renewed confidence filled me. For a moment, my cynical self had a vision of a lonely Yak herder, somewhere in Uzbekistan, selflessly offering his bitch, for all the good that would do, but optimism prevailed. When I went to sleep that night, my last thought was that the World Wide Web could have a connection waiting right around the corner.

34.
SCHUYLER THE SCHNAUZER RULER
CAROL HANSON

Schuyler was a miniature Schnauzer with a sister named Schatzi and a brother named Schnapps. Schuyler was the runt of the litter and the least sociable. He and his siblings were born at a Schnauzer breeding farm. There were a ton of dogs there. Most looked similar to him, which was salt and pepper, but it looked more like one big leaping and bounding field of Oreo's! He preferred that to being called a condiment!

Today someone was coming to choose between his brother and himself. Schuyler knew he should be putting on his best appearance so he would be chosen. The thing is though, he knew that he would have to commiserate with the other Schnauzers to look like the best choice. Schuyler retreated to the fence where he felt the most comfortable.

Pretty soon Callie came to pick out one of the pups. Schatzi was already promised to a family so it would be between Schnapps and him. Well, that was a 50% shot! Of course, Schnapps was *putting on the dog!*

Callie spotted Schuyler right away. *Holy S&H Green Stamps, she is looking right at me,* thought Schuyler. *This is going to be my lucky day!* He was alone and sitting at the fence, but Callie thought he didn't seem to want to be in the spotlight and wasn't even interacting with his litter mates. Schnapps, on the other hand, was in full puppy mode. It was kind of a no-brainer, and Callie picked Schnapps. Schuyler was bummed out but knew that he no longer had to compete. *For sure, the next people who came would have to choose me.*

Callie would not be able to take her dog home for another six weeks until he had been weaned. She made all the arrangements. She had Schnapps micro-chipped and asked that his ears be left alone. No cropping! About this she was adamant.

A couple of weeks after Callie purchased Schnapps, she received a phone call from the breeding farm. They told her they had mistakenly taken Schnapps and had his ears cut in the traditional Schnauzer style. Callie was so livid, she could have spit nails! She was not a happy camper! Time was of the essence to spend with her new dog before she had to resume her teaching job. She really needed that quality time to train him properly.

Callie decided to go out and visit Schuyler at the farm again. He was the only puppy that was available. She decided that she would grudgingly take him although her hostility was directed more at the breeding farm for making such a big mistake. When the time came, she put a box in the car and drove out to the farm. She put Schuyler lovingly in the box with a blanket and told him "Let me make myself perfectly clear. You are not the dog I paid for!" Schuyler looked at her as if to say "I've seen better homes than this crappy box, so we're even!"

When they got to Callie's, he realized that this was actually his new home. *Not bad digs at all!* Well, it took no time at all for Schuyler and Callie to bond. Schuyler turned out to be the best companion and friend Callie could ask for. It was now a running joke that when she got mad at Schuyler she would use that phrase again, as she did on that very first day. But in the end, she would give him a "high four!"

Schuyler is ten now, and a year ago he was diagnosed as being blind. No matter what, Callie and Schuyler will stick together through thick and thin. They were in for the long haul. To Callie, he would always be "Schuyler the Schnauzer Ruler."

SCHUYLER THE SCHNAUZER RULER
CAROL HANSON

35.
SHELTER ROOF, BLOODY FLOOR
PART TWO:
CANNIBALS VS. ZOMBIES
JENNIFER KOCH
Part one featured in Write to Woof 2014

Come find your next best friend. The sign's brick façade had crumbled away just a bit more since the last time he'd seen it. Yet, even though the letters had faded and chipped down to simple outlines over the years, he still read it from memory every time he crossed the barren parking lot towards the threshold of the Animals Welcome shelter.

Having suffered significant damage and looting during the troubles of the past eleven years, the building itself didn't look much better; yet, everyone who managed to stagger into their camp understood the importance of such a place and had helped to fix it up as best they could without power tools and modern conveniences. In this new world, despite looking as if it would collapse at any moment, the place held up well – maintaining the hope and humanity of their entire community.

Pulling open the door to the lobby, Bacon was careful to look around his ankles to be sure none of their four-legged friends got out into the big bad world on their own. A question greeted him instead, "Nothing?"

"Nothing," he replied, not looking up to see the frustration he knew would flash across Jason's face. This was the fourth time they'd been out and only run into the infected, the pups they couldn't save.

The sound of their voices caused a roar of barking to come from just behind the doors to the right of the lobby. The sound always made Bacon wondered how humans could have ever thought they could go on in life without the dependency and friendship of dogs.

When the infection had started to spread, people speculated that it came from dogs and many had been put down in an effort to stop it, but Bacon had always known that was just fear and ignorance. He knew humans and dogs would always need each other, that the phrase 'man's best friend' wasn't something to take lightly. The world had gone to hell around them, yet here they were—a small fraction of them anyways, still protecting and depending on each other for not only shared survival but also shared humanity. It all added up to a disappointed feeling in how dogs had long been whittled down to "just pets", where throwing a ball was done from a lawn chair and taking a walk was only to make sure they didn't pee on the carpet.

"We saw plenty of pups, put down as many as we could, but still..." Neither Bacon nor Jason turned to look at David, the newest member of their hunting party. It had been his first time out, his first time having to be the one to pull the trigger.

"You asked for the job David," Jason said, helping Bacon with his equipment.

"Yeah, and I wanna do it... doesn't make it right though."

"What about any of this is right?" Bacon asked sarcastically. "Still gotta do it." He threw the last of his things at David and laughed when he was given an annoyed look in return.

"We'll just have to find a new area to search next time, seems that section has been overrun. I'll send some teams out to flush out the rest of the pups and clean house. That should help our friends reclaim things."

Jason, ever the army sergeant, always took charge of things. He'd been the one to come up with all the plans, all the slang to distinguish between the infected "pups" and their healthy "friends" —the dogs they relied on to help protect their small settlement from all the things that now haunted both the dark and the daylight.   David was the exact opposite, a naïve kid who'd only been about seven when the troubles first started.   He was one of a handful among them that still referred to the infected as zombies, having been exposed to the term incessantly while the media outlets were all still up and running. Most people still standing, including Bacon, had never cared what it was or what it was called—they only cared about surviving. And, these days, that meant having man's best friend always at your side.

It hadn't taken long for people to notice that dogs could sense the illness in others before it even appeared. The scent, the behavior, the look in their eyes... the healthy dogs just knew when something wasn't right; they relied on the signals that humans had long forgotten. It had been a joke at first, with those who thought traveling with a dog was a waste of supplies and energy scoffing at those who did. But, their tunes changed quickly enough... if they managed to survive. Bacon had always been a dog man, having at least one since he was a boy.   His namesake, Bacon, had been the dog he'd had when everything first started to get serious. Bacon had saved his life on many occasions before finally being taken down by age. Bacon took on the name in remembrance, finding his old one to be unfitting of the current life he now led.

In that same state of mind, he'd come across Animals Welcome and the few remaining healthy dogs that still gathered there.   It took some convincing, and plenty of his food stores, to get the dogs to trust him, but eventually things grew into the community they had now. Hundreds of people depend on him and the healthy friends he was able to return with to protect them and maintain the only comforts they had left. Treating them as pets wasn't even something they thought of anymore, they were equals.

"Sorry guys, no new friends today." David's words only barely register within Bacon's thoughts, but it was enough to pull him out of his melancholy reminiscence.

He watched David pull open one of the side doors that lead deeper into the shelter and knew the lobby would quickly be flooded with dogs of all sizes, each greeting them as if they had been gone for months rather than days. Upon emerging, several of them ran straight to Bacon. David mockingly scowled, "They always like you best."

"His name is Bacon," Jason called from his spot behind the counter, failing to do any map checking as a large Dalmatian propped himself up next to him and nudged his arm until he succeeded in getting a scratch behind the ears. "Now, if only we had some bacon, right buddy?"

Bacon gave him a sideways glance while David continued to play with the dogs, being too young to really remember what bacon was. "What are you trying to say there Jason?" he asked.

"Well, they do say that humans taste like pork..." Jason cracked a wicked smile.

David looked up at this and gave him a grossed-out look, "How the heck do you know that? ...You didn't..."

His voice showed his hesitation. Bacon gave Jason a smirk; both had been waiting for this moment. It was one they always looked forward to with the younger members of their camp, the ones too young to get the joke until after they'd had some fun – something that was in very short supply.

"Well, you know there are a lot of cannibals out there, right?" Jason started. "Like fighting off zombies wasn't bad enough, we gotta be worried about being eaten by those crazies too."

"Stop talking about it, that stuff still gives me nightmares," David protested.

"Yeah, it really makes you wonder which would be worse. Come on, David, cannibals versus zombies? Which one would you pick?" Bacon had to bite his lip to keep from laughing at David's pained expression.

"What is wrong with you two? How can you ask someone that?"

"But, wouldn't that solve a bunch of problems? You know, maybe the cannibals have the right idea. I could really go for some bacon right now," Jason mused, mockingly giving Bacon a salivating smirk.

The Dalmatian at his side let out an approving bark. "Oh geez, thanks to you too," Bacon responded incredulously as Jason happily scratched the dog behind the ears.

"That's right; you remember that bacon tastes good, don't you?" Jason teased. "Hey what'da say we take Bacon out back and grill up something yummie?"

Bacon glanced at David, who was looking at Jason as if he'd lost his mind. "You can't be serious... Bac... he's joking, right? You don't... did something happen while we..."

Bacon couldn't take it anymore; he fell to his knees in fits of laughter while Jason just laid his head on the counter in front of him, his laughter muffled by the Dalmatian sniffing around his head. It took a while for them to calm down, but when they finally did, they found David standing with his arms crossed. "Alright, what's so damn funny?"

Jason came around the counter and put his arm across David's shoulders, still chuckling slightly, "The look on your face..." David pushed him off.

"You're young; you wouldn't remember this great invention we used to have called movies. Back when people had time to daydream, they would come up with all sorts of things..."

Jason interrupted Bacon and gesticulated, "Yeah, we saw pink elephants, pigs could fly, and we found out that humans taste like bacon."

David, remembering movies just fine from all the TV he used to watch as a child, finally understood what was happening, "You guys are assholes."

Having succeeded in their prank, Bacon and Jason broke down again. This time, Bacon fell all the way to the floor in his fits of laughter and was immediately swarmed by the dogs who roamed freely around them. The large Dalmatian pushed his way through and lathered Bacon's face with several slobbery licks. "Hey, we were only joking," he laughed. "We're not really gonna eat me!"

"I don't know, you did get their hopes up," David remarked, getting his own revenge.

"Well, what'da know? He's got a sense of humor, after all," Jason grinned.

Bacon sat up and roughhoused with the Dalmatian, "Yeah, he'll fit right in."

Humans and dogs have long had an entwined codependence; even in the darkest times, we lighten each other's hearts. No matter what happens in life, remember that your four-legged friends aren't just pets, they're family.

36.
SHEPHERD
JOHN C. MANNONE

Max, a Border collie, with his long-nose
instincts, would watch over our house,
protecting it from wolves—neighborhood
thieves—while anxiously waiting
for my return.

Every time I got out of the car,
he'd herd me like the sheep he never saw,
corral me towards the car, away
from the front door, keeping me with him
a little while longer. I became the lamb.
His eyes would lock on mine, speaking
without "words" but with a gate-keeper-smile,
the brown shimmer of his eyes, still
as spring water.

37.
SILENCE
DENNIS KLOTZ

Ever since I was young, I've been a dog person. I've always preferred them to cats, perhaps in part, due to my cat allergies. Though dogs have a reputation for being more boisterous and outgoing than cats, Pumper, the family Dalmatian that I had growing up, and Pepper, the miniature Dachshund I have now, both reflected my more introverted personality and were both highly attuned to my emotions.

Due to a physical disability called Arthrogryposis, I had several surgeries as a child and I was frequently in a lot of pain. I remember Pumper always being very concerned and protective of me, whether watching me while I crawled around or coming by to lick my face when I was crying in pain. In the autumn, when my father raked the leaves into big piles, she would play with me in the leaves and Pumper and I would pass the afternoon outside. Dalmatians sometimes can be territorial and aggressive, but Pumper was neither. She was a very peaceful dog. They are also known for their spots, but she had hardly any. In addition to her lack of spots, she had one blue eye and one brown eye. She wasn't your average Dalmatian, but I wasn't the average child, and in a sense I felt like we understood each other better because of it.

I remember when she was older and having problems controlling her bladder, and her being confused why we were upset with her. She didn't have a way to voice her needs or her pain, and I remember feeling sad that she couldn't. When we had to put her down, I remember hugging her for the last time and I wish she knew how much I loved her. But I think she understood, even though she couldn't speak.

Shortly after Pumper, my parents got a black miniature Dachshund. They let me name him, and I named him Pepper. Even as a puppy, he was quiet; so quiet that my father accidentally stepped on him because he didn't know he was there. The vet said it was the equivalent of getting hit by a car. He hurt his ribs and was on medication for a while, but he was okay. After that, we put a bell on him so we could always hear where he was. Even with a bell, his personality shown through, as he was always jingling at a leisurely pace through the house. He was wild as a puppy, doing all of the things you expect of puppies; chasing birds, playing with toys, guarding bones, and barking at every passerby and car. I used to take him for walks around the neighborhood. Longer walks than my parents took him on. Pepper and I walked all over, even getting lost well past twilight one night.

I remember his first winter. We took him up with us to the family cabin, and it was the first time he experienced snow. He loved it, and he and I ran up the snow banks and made boot and paw prints in the fresh snow. In the summer, when we took him to the cabin, he loved going in the water, and his little paws would start kicking before we even set him down in it. He would bark and swim towards the ducks, only to be confused when they flew away as he grew near. On one of his beach adventures, he took off down the beach and we chased him down, hoping he wouldn't break for the woods beyond. We lost sight of him at one point, only to find him paws deep in quicksand. We rescued him after twenty minutes of getting him unstuck, but it wasn't the first time he ran away. He broke loose at the hotel once, and the manager, two desk clerks, and even the chef were chasing him through the parking lot with my parents and me, trying to block off cars, all of us praying that he wouldn't try to run into the busy intersection. When we finally trapped him between some cars, we were relieved, but he still didn't learn his lesson. We left him in the room the next time, but he chewed at the carpet and we decided that his hotel days were over.

As adventurous as Pepper was, he was also a pretty reserved dog. I remember many summer afternoons and winter evenings curled up on the couch with a good book, him on my lap, the both of us drifting into sleep.

When he got older, I noticed a change in him. He was starting to slow down and sometimes he would yelp in pain. Dachshunds are known to have back problems due to their long spine, and although he always sat up to beg for food, his problems were not with his back, but with his hip. He didn't run as much, and he no longer would run down the stairs, leaping the last few steps like Super Dog. He grew tired quicker on walks, and he stopped playing with his toys. We put him on medication, but he was still not as active as he was in his younger days.

There was also a change happening with me as well. The depression that I have had all throughout my life had worsened, and although I am naturally introverted, I had kept most of it to myself. Some days when I felt especially alone, I would cry. Pepper would perk his head up and look at me and I remembered that I wasn't so alone, after all.

It was one of those days where everything felt like it was going wrong, and I was especially distraught. I felt a lump in my throat, and I sat in silence. It was then that I heard it. It was a small whimper. Pepper was sleeping on the couch, and every now and again he would whimper and groan. I remembered something I had read about depression being common in older dogs, and I knew that I wasn't the only one who suffered in silence. He had pain and sadness just like me. I sat there, watching him sleep a while, listening again to him snore. I wondered what he was dreaming about. Maybe he was dreaming of being a puppy, dreaming of being young again. He whimpered again in his sleep and then I started to cry. But they were not tears of pain or sorrow. They were tears of happiness. I was happy that I had a friend who understood me, who was going through what I was going through, who loved me unconditionally, and who was there to support me, without even saying a word. Because sometimes there is a compassion that words cannot express. I went over and petted him for a while as he slept. He woke up briefly and looked at me. I wanted to tell him how much I love him and how much I care about him. I wanted to thank him for being there for me through everything. I wanted to thank him for all of the memories we shared together. He only wagged his tail and then went back to his dog dreams. I think he understood.

38.
STILL THERE
KAGE ALAN

There are some who believe that we come into this life destined to meet up with an animal companion who has been with us before and may yet be with us again. It's actually a relief it's an animal and not, say, a Grandmonster-in-law. I have one of those. Believe me, an animal is a Godsend compared to the alternative. Now, we don't know which animal it will be, but we always know it upon reflection and after the time has passed. It's not a mystical revelation or Jedi thing. We just don't think about it during our time with the animal. It's only after the animal's passing that we hum the theme to *The X-Files* and add additional meaning to its life. And not that I don't already know there aren't any Jedi in *The X-Files*. Well, that we know about.

Moving along, I was once an absolutely adorably cute four-year-old boy with bleach blonde hair, blue eyes, and no siblings. This meant that while I didn't have to share anything, I also got the blame for everything regardless of whether or not I did it. And I did do it. I just didn't have anybody else to pin it on. So there I was... alone, needing, wanting, and watching cartoons without a companion to share the Moments with.

My parents used to take me to the mall during those first years and have me walk my little legs off. It apparently gave them some peace of mind that I'd wear myself out and go to bed that evening without putting up much of a fight. I wasn't fond of having a bedtime. Hey, when you want to stay up late and watch *The Streets of San Francisco*, one needs a little more for a reason to obey other than a parent merely saying "no." Anyway, we happened to be at Eastland Mall that day, back when it was actually safe to shop there, and wandered into the pet store. There, three-quarters of the way down the row of cages and towards the top—my father had to lift me up and let me sit on his shoulders—was the most incredible black and white puppy with eyes bluer than my own.

She didn't have a name, but there was a card on her cage Dad read to us; "Siberian Husky." Those words should have been enough to strike fear in our hearts because anybody who knows anything about Siberian Huskies understands that these little minions of mischief and mayhem are the cheerleaders of the dog world.   They're cute, they know it, and they have a lifetime of reminding you of it ahead of them. You don't open your home to one.   Rather, you have been getting their home ready for the day they walk through the door and assume control over the household.   That's a Husky.

We had no intention of getting a dog that day or any other in the foreseeable future. Something clicked, though. There was a connection and Dad saw it. Mom didn't. I did. Mom still didn't. Dad thought we should get her. Mom didn't. I wanted a dog. Mom still didn't. I could be wrong. Mom might have been all for it, but that really doesn't do much for building suspense, does it? Suffice to say we did buy her and written at the top of her papers were the words "Kage's Dog".

I don't remember if we waited, bought her that same day, or had to wait to pick her up after paying for her. I'm a little foggy on that. I do recall sitting in the back seat of my parents' black gas guzzling Charger, opening a cardboard box from the store, and her bursting out of it, full of vim and vigor and ready to play. I remember that very clearly.

The name my folks decided upon was Tashka. My father's nickname for her over the years was Snicklefritz.

It's not an insult or disservice to my mother to say that she and Tashka didn't get along particularly well in the beginning. Tashka wanted to chew on everything—that was the puppy in her—and didn't respond well to the word "no" or attempts to train her—that was that Husky in her. It didn't help that our new family member suffered from colitis. I was really too young to help much and Dad worked all kinds of hours, so Mom was taking up all the slack when she herself wasn't working. This created a somewhat 'grrrrrrr' atmosphere in the house.

Things did escalate to the point where Mom put her foot down and told my father "Either the dog goes or I go." Dad believed in patience and logic. My mother believed in exorcising the house of this shedding, chewing menace to her psychological well-being. Dad replied with a simple "Then pack your bags." Yes, he called my mother's bluff. Fortunately, Mom didn't play Poker. Crazy Eights? Yes. Poker? No. But Tashka was relegated to living in the basement.

A funny thing happened a couple of months later, though. Dad used to go up north and do what he called 'hunting'. I use that term loosely because he never caught anything. Oh, he went in the woods and he even took his bow and arrows, only I'm convinced after years of getting to know the man that he just sat there and watched the wildlife around him. He enjoyed it. It may also have been the only peace and quiet he ever got. Mom, meanwhile, was stuck at home with both myself and Tashka. It was during a hunting trip when Dad was away that Mom thought she heard someone outside the house and panicked. Dad came back home and discovered Tashka had moved upstairs into their room. On their bed. And she and Mom were acting as if there'd never been any tension.

Huskies are a bit fickle when it comes to love. When they want the attention, you'll know it. And if you don't give it to them, you'll hear about it. Bend down to pet one who doesn't want the attention and they'll bend down even farther to avoid your hand, get up, walk away, and give you a side look that suggests you'd better ask first next time before thinking you can just touch one of them. Worst of all, if you have company, Huskies will monopolize your guests' time and regale them with all the woes they are forced to endure, especially the poor service they receive from family members. It can get a little embarrassing.

Our second Husky was particularly vocal about these things. But Tashka? Not so much. The only thing she was known for with company is if she didn't deem your presence acceptable, she'd lean in, make you think she was going to give you a kiss, then sneeze on you. This delighted my little sister with fur to no end and left us scrambling to warn company before they were greeted with an unpleasant surprise. Or, if we were too late, hand them a tissue... or two.

Tashka and I tended to act like siblings. We both craved parental attention, both wanted dessert, and both wanted to be first at the front door when Dad walked in from work. I would be playing in my bedroom at the end of the hall and Tashka would be taking a nap in my parents' room across from my own. We'd hear the front door open and both of us would make a beeline for it. I wanted to get there first. So did she. I wasn't a sore loser. She was. If I was in the lead, she refused to stay behind me or try to pass me on the left or the right. Instead, she'd run between my legs and flip me up in the air. Nobody could convince me at the time that she wasn't trying to kill me.

We were in sync much of the rest of the time, however. I wasn't fond of breakfast sausage and Tashka was. I'd eat just enough to make my folks think I was going to finish it, then start slipping bits of it under the table to a waiting mouth. In this, we got along famously. On a more playful side, one of us couldn't walk past the other without taking a swipe at each other or nudging each other out of the way. Tashka would make her displeasure known, thereby prompting Mom to yell at me and separate us. My folks would then laugh as my little beast of burden would crawl towards me an inch at a time, egging me on to play with her some more.

Another game we had is I'd point a finger at Tashka... and she'd smile. Actually, she'd bare her teeth and she did look quite ferocious, only it truly was a game between us. It didn't matter if I was sitting right in front of her or fifteen feet away. I'd raise my hand, and then extend my finger at her and she'd bare her teeth. I'd retract my finger and her mouth relaxed. Unfortunately, people who didn't know about this game panicked a little when they pointed and Tashka smiled. Our house vet was highly unamused one particular afternoon when he visited and commanded her to sit, which was accompanied with a finger point. Tashka smiled. The vet almost had a movement in his pants. Fortunately, Mom jumped in and quickly explained things, but that didn't stop him from giving me a lecture about not teaching a dog such a horrible thing. He also didn't appreciate my response; "It's not polite to point."

The world around me got a little bigger when I turned twelve and took my first plane ride. Dad's aunt and uncle invited me to stay with them for a week in California and that was an experience I've never forgotten. Upon coming home, though, I couldn't help but notice that things seemed smaller to me than they had before, even Tashka. It was a strange turning point in my life, but one of growing up. I was getting older and Tashka was getting older.

There was a retirement complex along the route where Mom and I would walk Tashka each day. Mom would hand the leash over to me when we got to the complex's driveway, then Tashka and I would run around the back of the place while Mom continued along the sidewalk and met us at the other end. The runs gradually became jogs, trots, and then just our regular walking speed. It was Tashka's and my part of the walk, but while I was approaching the pinnacle of my youth, she was approaching old age.

Tashka developed arthritis in her lower spine and she struggled to keep her back legs upright when she walked. Cortisone shots helped, but there was no cure. Going down the stairs remained manageable for her, but she needed help going back up and I can't recall ever complaining, even in jest, assisting her. I didn't have genetic siblings and there were times I didn't even have friends, but I always had her. Tashka had been with me longer than I'd been without her.

Endings hold a certain fascination for me because there can sometimes be a certain symmetry to them. Tashka came into my life when I needed a companion. She became a welcome addition to the family and an extension of my soul. Fourteen years later, I would be graduating from high school, spending six weeks in Germany, and then starting college on the other side of the state, essentially deserting her. It felt like a cruel thing to do to someone who'd been with me for so long. Maybe she knew change was at our doorstep, though, and that this change had to happen. It was the natural progression of life; some things ended, some things continued, and some things began.

Tashka's quality of life had reached a point two weeks before I graduated from high school that required us to make a decision. It was the first time I'd been faced with having to help decide—at least in this capacity—what was best for someone versus my own feelings of what was best for me regarding them. Wasn't there anything else we could do to make Tashka healthier? Anything at all? Some medical treatment we didn't know about? Something? Anything? No.

It was one of the better spring mornings I can recall. The temperature was comfortable, a soft breeze blew the scent of honeysuckle and lily of the valley, and there was a nice layer of dew on the freshly cut grass outside. The sun was shining, too. Nothing outside hinted at what was planned a short time later. Tashka relished the extra treats we'd given her the past couple of days and still enjoyed walking around outside where she'd played for fourteen years. This day was no different, but she did look tired. I think I have pictures Mom took from that morning.

The house vet arrived and was somber instead of his usual lecturing self. I helped Tashka up into the back of our van where she'd spent time when we'd taken her up north with us or on other trips. She laid down, then Mom, Dad, and I all held her. The vet shaved part of her leg, found the vein he needed, and readied the injection. He assured us again it would be painless and that it was the humane thing to do. Even I realized it was time. We told Tashka we loved her, and then the vet gave her the shot.

Something unexpected happened at this point, something that shocked even the vet. Tashka howled. I don't believe it was because of physical pain, though. She howled because I think she realized what was happening and didn't want to leave. I sat there, holding her, and listened to her final howl. And as the sound of her howl died down, she slipped away from us until what remained, the shell, was at peace and motionless.

I remember staring at the vet, tears streaming down my face, and screaming "I thought you said it wouldn't hurt?" at him. It was unfair of me—he was just as upset as we were—but he didn't get angry or hold it against me. He knew. He'd done this before and he knew the emotions involved. I bolted from the van and retreated to my bedroom.

Dad drove her to a place to have her cremated. Mom stayed home with me, only we stayed away from each other. We wanted to mourn in our own way and we both knew if one of us started to cry, the other would quickly follow. Dad returned and when I went outside to do something, I found him standing up against the back gate. It was the only time I've ever seen my father cry.

A friend at school the following week found out what had happened and wordlessly gave me a hug and a flower in Tashka's memory. I graduated two weeks later, spent six weeks in Germany that summer, and started college at Grand Valley State University in the fall. Tashka's ashes remain at my parents' house next to other dogs my family has opened their home to since. It's my wish that one day, when my time has come, my ashes will be mixed with my husband's and Tashka's, then spread out together somewhere. Maybe up north on some spring morning when the sun is out and there's a layer of dew on the grass.

Or, if my husband's Grandmonster is still alive—evil entities live to be over 150 years old, don't they?—she could spread us all out on a windy day where a sudden gust blows us right back towards her and makes her sneeze. There's symmetry there, too.

Tashka has never strayed far from my mind or heart and I can still see her and feel her presence around me in life. There have been times during the past twenty-seven years when I've been asleep and heard—even felt—Tashka jump up on my bed, turn a circle or two, and lay down. I typically wake up because I'm a little unnerved at first. That shortly gives way to realizing who it was, and I settle right back down knowing she's still checking up on me, still there.

STILL THERE
KAGE ALAN

39.
THE GIRLFRIEND
CHERYL GILLESPIE

She was Bode's girlfriend first.   Powder bounded into our dog Bode's life when he was five years old.   She was the new, light-yellow female Lab of the neighbors who live diagonally from us in our rural section of a town just north of the only city of any size in southern Maine, or all of Maine in reality.   An adorable puppy, she squirmed and yapped and charmed everyone, including Bode.   Our sweet, male dog, a cinnamon yellow as the result of a yellow father and chocolate mother, had proven himself to be a nonaggressive lover whom neighbors were not afraid of in spite of being eighty pounds.   For the first three years of his life, he was the patient companion of my elderly father-in-law who found the dog lead on our back deck too much of a hassle to deal with and would let Bode out to roam free while my husband and I were at work. Fortunately, sweet Bode endeared himself to the neighbors who were home during the day and did not journey far.   Bode adored little kids and puppies.   He loved my father-in-law and missed him dreadfully when he left us.   Bode was infatuated with Powder immediately.

A trail already existed through the woods between Powder's house and ours since our daughters had blazed it to run up to a dear neighborhood lady who often babysat them for us.   In fact, the path had been christened Mrs. Brown Avenue after this lovely person. Coffee and muffins had ceremoniously been enjoyed after the sign was nailed up with her name on it. When the girls grew too old to travel the avenue to the sitter, Bode and Powder made good use of it. One can still stand at our end of the path, easily see both our house and Powder's, and shout back and forth. We checked on the two dogs' whereabouts in this manner.

At first the love affair between Bode and Powder was somewhat lopsided. Bode would lie on the lawn and let Powder jump all over him and chew his ears without a sign of complaint. Powder grew swiftly into a beautiful little female Lab, who could run and play with Bode. Even though she always acted submissive toward him, he would occasionally knock her on her side and soft chew her neck. She seemed to love this and would tease him until he did this time and again. They spent hours together. We live in a housing development where the lots are two acres or more with sections of woods purposely left untouched when houses were built, so it is an ideal dog neighborhood. Although many neighbors had decided to install invisible fences, Powder's owners and we had decided to be the rebels who claimed our Labs were under "voice control," and we didn't bother with such devices. Bode and Powder were free spirits.

These two canine characters shared everything. Powder brought over every ball that her child owners played with and any other dog toy she could find. If Bode was off with us when Powder visited, she would leave a ball on our steps as her calling card. Powder also grabbed and scooted home with any of Bode's toys she decided she liked. One Christmas I fussed to my husband about being hesitant to buy Bode a holiday toy since Powder would probably steal it anyway. Shortly after making that statement, I watched Bode scurry through the woods path to Powder's house with a toy and come back without it. He obviously did not mind sharing.

Both pups loved the snow. I have pictures of the two of them lying side by side on a snow bank grinning at the world. In the summer, they carved grooves at the corners of the lawn around our house while they were running circles after one another. Leaf piles were joyfully knocked down by them in the fall. Newly planted spring annuals did not fare well when they played nearby. One of their absolute delights was an old stainless steel salad bowl filled with fresh water and left for them on the back steps.

Rambunctious play would be followed by loud slurping and panting at that water spot.

The standing joke between Powder's owners and us was that we had to tell one another if we were going to be away for more than just the day. It was painful to watch Bode sit at the atrium door at the back deck and watch for Powder and cry when she didn't show up. They claimed Powder missed Bode, too if he was away for any length of time.

About a year and a half ago, Bode's arthritis became more and more severe. Though supplements, muscle relaxers, and painkillers were introduced, he gradually found it impossible to keep up with his soulmate. He would simply watch and smile as she ran for a ball we threw. Powder adapted. She would run around him and keep stopping to nuzzle and tease him.

Bode's progression to a disabled, old pooch seemed to happen fast. He soon moved slowly and with difficulty, but Powder always visited. She would perch in front of him and shower his face with licks until he seemed impatient with her, but he would always look for her. Canine chiropractic treatments and massages helped some until the day a disc in his back slipped to the point where he was paralyzed. After talk of peripheral damage rendering surgery a bad option, the vet advised us to let him go. That was a few months ago.

The snow on Mrs. Brown Avenue is still beaten down. Powder visits as often as usual. At first she smelled around the house and gave us accusing glares, but she still sat on the kitchen rug and waited for her dog treats. As time went on, she stopped her search and simply greeted my husband and me with affectionate licks and her infectious smile. Although her visits sometimes tug at our hearts with memories of our Bode, they also soothe us. There is nothing like a dog to heal one's pain. I still buy boxes of dog treats when I grocery shop. Though Bode was Powder's first love, we realize Powder is our girlfriend, too.

THE GIRLFRIEND
CHERYL GILLESPIE

40.
THE TRACKER
ELISABETH WARD

Depressions in moist grass behind him
  show where his nose reads last night's stories,
  searching sequels in the early light.

I need that light to see his path
  where weight, so solid on long slim legs,
  spreads wide pads yet wider when he runs.

It's all so clear to him in his pursuit,
  like the rabbit held before a greyhound,
  while I must stop, observe and feel the air

Left in his wake. Later, stretched across the floor
  beside my feet, eyes closed, nose twitching,
  his legs still churn in memory of what I've yet to find

As I sift stories of my day, chase down soft
  impressions and reduce that time to words
  upon a page.

Previous publication in the chapbook Naked Weimaraner: The Dogs,
The Cats, The Rest, Shaggy Dog Press, 2005

41.
TWO DOGS AND THEN SOME
MICHAELEEN KELLY

Frodo stands too close to the ground
To be exuding such majesty
In his medieval green velvet waistcoat
Encasing his silky white fur
Accentuating the chasm between his royal demeanor
And his plaintive look of wonderment
"Is this all there is? Am I really just a dog?"
We need Frodo to be asking the question
So we can postpone and deflect our own meager responses.

If we gave Sable a rat to chase down
And constructed sundry obstacles
Between her and her prey
She would electrify the house
With her breakneck speed
And pinpointed accuracy
Providing us with catharsis
When she rids our world
Of another unwelcome varmint.

"Frodo and Sable look like they want to get married".
Maybe so
Maybe they haven't reached their comfort zone
Of domestic singles cohabitation.

Body transforming existential angst
A chase to the death
Primal pre-marital coupling
Is this all there is?

42.
UNTIL HE ARRIVES
MATT MCGEE

Alicia was a tan buxom beauty with nowhere to go. Her father had left her a small adobe house thirty miles into the New Mexico desert—broken windows, rattling screen door, warped floorboards and all. There was no heat, no power, just a forty-year-old Ford pick-up to carry her to town if needed, and she rarely needed, and her old yellow lab to keep her company. And there was the gun. Papi had seen to that.

Alicia didn't mind the heat, it made her skin tingle with little pricks of light she was sure were spearing through the roof, slipping past the blowing curtains on cracked windows that kept out almost nothing. She spent most of her time lying in bed, or on the old ratty couch she shared with her dog Boo, the yellow lab that drank more water than she did. Alicia wondered to herself if the dog was diabetic like her father had been, or if he was just, well, thirsty.

Buried in an anonymous patch of heated desert she didn't care to leave or even roam, when she pressed her ear to the floor at night and listened she could hear two things: a rumble she was sure came from the tires of passing semis over a mile away; *though*, she thought, *maybe it was the rushing of blood in my head.*

And she heard the coyotes. She loved the coyotes. People in towns and cities didn't understand them. They were lonely. They were survivors. Alicia would lie on the floor by day avoiding the heat, and feeling the sun weaken, she would wait for the cooled air to blow through the rusted screens. It was a welcome relief after another baking day, and with the breeze came the woo of the mongrel dogs.

She was lying in bed one day; it was early still, before noon. She was still naked, unwashed from the night before. Heat rose, so she flopped out of bed onto the floor beside Boo, who was smart enough to know the old wood floor would be cooler. She pressed her ear to the wood, coated in more dirt than she knew.

"You can hear them down here, Boo." The dog opened its eyes and twitched a brow her way, then went back to resting.

"You can hear the trucks." Alicia pressed her ear to the warped floor, harder still. She imagined she could tell the trucks by their tires: BF Goodriches, Goodyears, huge black rubber donuts like those she'd swung on as a kid when they lived in town. It seemed every house had a swing made of tire and rope, a small fence to keep the kids in sight and a vigilant dog to keep an eye when parents stepped away.

Alicia pushed herself up off the floor and stepped toward the window. It wasn't as hot today. She slid aside the lace curtain, stained by sun and dust, and peered out across the acres no one wanted, or for all she knew, no one even knew existed. But there must be someone—there must somewhere be a man who wanted to come here, swoop her up and bring her to a place with fountains and vines climbing the walls, where palm trees were the only shade and servants roamed around.

Alicia stood staring out the window, dreaming, when her eyes caught something moving across the yard. It was pale, whitish, rolling like a tumbleweed about twenty feet away. She slipped on her old shoes and dashed into the yard, bare as the Earth that had bore her, Boo close behind wondering what the adventure was. She and the dog chased the paper until Alicia could snatch it up with one hand.

She stood in the center of the yard, holding the tattered pages of the mass-produced magazine. Boo sniffed, hoping as usual for something to eat, drink, or chase. Alicia was studying the pages, or what was left of them when Boo let out a growl; Alicia looked up to the horizon and scanned around until her eyes landed on the small body of a canine, almost hidden by brush, spying on her and Boo from a safe distance.

"Are you the boy who calls me at night?"

The coyote stared. It listened as Alicia howled. Then it turned and moved away, slinking back over the horizon.

"Typical man."

Alicia carried the worn, dry magazine back toward the house. It was over a year old and, by her guess, must have blown quite some time before it finally reached her. Maybe the mailman back on the road had dropped it. She hadn't seen him in months. No one wrote to her anymore and no one called. Even the letters from the real estate people had stopped. They knew she wouldn't sell. She didn't know how and she wouldn't have anywhere to go, anyway.

Alicia lay back on her bed, flinging her hair up over the top of her pillow. She wasn't the world's fastest reader but this wasn't the world's greatest magazine, mostly large color photos of celebrities exiting expensive nightclubs or coming from lunch somewhere that always seemed to have palm trees nearby. She wondered how celebrities could afford to eat so much. She only ate when she was hungry and even then, what little she had she shared with Boo.

Her eyes flickered with excitement as she took in all the pictures, until one handsome, tanned man named Matthew Mac-something, she couldn't pronounce his last name appeared on page forty-seven. He wore a light beige suit the color of sand and was in mid-stride when the photographer took his picture. Alicia had never seen him before, but he seemed to walk like he owned the world, and as the sun settled outside her window that night, she went on imagining that he was indeed a king or some royalty that ruled a distant world from his palm tree-lined estate, tucked in a desert like hers and not far away.

She slowly let her eyes roll shut, and when she slept, Alicia saw herself wrapped in the kind of sheer garment that barely covered her. She lay atop a chaise lounge and listened to Matthew command the servants of their palm-lined estate; she imagined giving orders with the flick of a wrist, dismissing this one, telling that one to fetch her something cold to eat or drink, to tend the grounds so she wouldn't have to. Then Matthew would relax upon his throne, arms resting by his sides, satisfied with the wife he had found on a trip through the desert, living alone with only an old dog to keep her company. She had pointed a gun at him at first but lowered it when she recognized him from a magazine photo. With his Texas charm, he talked her into some clothes, into his limousine and to another life in a mild climate, to watch over a palace that met everything she ever imagined. He had swooped her up, carried her in those tan, solid arms and brought her here, to their palm-lined oasis, where she would be his wife and serve him in ways she had only imagined being useful to a man.

Alicia was deep into her fantasy when the first coyote of the night echoed through her window, piercing the broken glass and entering her room. And she leaned her head back, aroused; wanting Matthew to come now, to take her away from a loneliness only she, an old Ford, and a vigilant loyal dog knew existed.

UNTIL HE ARRIVES
MATT MCGEE
"Wolfgirl" Illustration by Ashley McMillian

43.
WHAT THE DOG KNOWS
HUGH ANDERSON

The full moon shreds clouds and bares stars
in patches. Rain has stopped, but flecks of wet
swarm like gnats under the streetlights.
We walk the middle of the street, dog alert,
houses hunkered down against the storm
just past. From the unlit playground, the sound
of voices, the flat *plok* of a kicked ball.

I am blind to what the dog knows of the wind.
Her hackles rise, she stops. Two deer
rise on the steep lawn above, watch us,
shadow ears twitching. I give the leash a shake,
and she trots on, white tip of her tail a beacon.
Nostrils flare as she reads the air. Her hair
still bristles. The burly wind, impatient,

elbows branches aside. Weighted by the gravity
of the freight it carries, it staggers down the street.
Dog strains at its trail, and I, on the slow end
of the leash, am dragged into
a message
I cannot comprehend.

44.
WHEN MY CHIHUAHUA SLEEPS
A.J. HUFFMAN

He becomes one with the blanket,
twists and turns until his body disappears
into red satin folds. Just another wrinkle,
you would not even know he was
there except for the tiny black nose,
the four white whiskers barely peeking
from beneath fabric's hem.

45.
WITH HOOVERING
A.J. HUFFMAN

tongue, my puppy sweeps couch and crevice
for crumbs of elicit human food otherwise denied.
Salted and sweetened trails, invisible to my eyes,
draw him under table and cushions, into corners
and cracks barely accessible to the adeptness
of his consumptive organ. Inevitably, he resurfaces,
sated by whatever magical morsel he managed
to maneuver into his mouth.

CONTRIBUTING AUTHORS
"RED THE WONDER PUPPY"
VICTORIA SCOTT

A.J. HUFFMAN

A.J. HUFFMAN

Where are you from?
Ormond Beach, Florida.

Describe in one or two sentences how being friends with a dog has enriched your life.
My dog, Icarus, keeps me sane. He sits at my feet when I am working, and seems to know when I'm stressing. He puts his head on my feet to remind me that he's there and that he loves me, no matter what. Makes whatever issue I'm dealing with seem much less draining.

Do you have any other pets; if so, what are their breeds and names?
My sister also has a dog, named Bumper. My sister and Bumper moved in last year and now the two dogs are inseparable. You'd think they were from the same litter.

If you are a writer (either by trade or compulsion) what first drew you to the craft? If you're not a writer, why did you choose to write a piece for this anthology?
I started writing in grade school. It's just something I've always done, but I did not decide on it as a career until I was in college. It was the only thing I could see myself doing for the rest of my life.

ALEXANDRA HEEP

ALEXANDRA HEEP

Where are you from?

I was born and raised in Germany. I moved to the USA at age 18 in 1986. I have lived in Michigan and Virginia, before settling in Chicago, Illinois.

Describe in one or two sentences how being friends with a dog has enriched your life.

Adrianne Bonnie, the Dachshund, came with my boyfriend. I always thought that cats and dogs could not live together peacefully, but amazingly, "his" dog and "my" cat get along well. Of course now they are both "our" pets or should I say, we are theirs.

Do you have any other pets; if so, what are their breeds and names?

We also have a tabby cat named Princess Gracie, who appears in the 2014 Write to Meow Anthology.

If you are a writer (either by trade or compulsion) what first drew you to the craft? If you're not a writer, why did you choose to write a piece for this anthology?

First I became a writer out of passion and to see if I could compete with native-English writers, then the craft turned into necessity when I was laid off and became ill. It was the option for survival.

https://www.linkedin.com/in/alexandraheep

ALISA NORRIS

Where are you from?
Bloomfield Hills, Michigan.

Describe in one or two sentences how being friends with a dog has enriched your life.
I don't remember a time when I was growing up where my family didn't have a dog around. Dogs shower you with unconditional love and constant companionship. They seem to have an innate ability to sense your needs. If you are sad, they know how to comfort you with just a knowing look. If you are lonely, they will curl up next to you. And if you are happy, they're the happiest right along with you.

Do you have any other pets; if so, what are their breeds and names?
Rollo, Yorkie/Chihuahua mix; Reese, Yorkie/Toy Fox Terrier mix and star of the story.

If you are a writer (either by trade or compulsion) what first drew you to the craft? If you're not a writer, why did you choose to write a piece for this anthology?
I write because I enjoy being able to get inside someone else's head, even a fictional one, and see what they see. I love to watch how my characters deal with difficult situations or squirm with the uncomfortable ones.

CARLA MARIA VERDINO-SÜLLWOLD

CARLA MARIA VERDINO-SÜLLWOLD

Where are you from?
I was born in Weehawken, New Jersey; have lived in the New York and Chicago metropolitan areas, and traveled the world on journalism and classical music assignments before settling in Brunswick, Maine.

Describe in one or two sentences how being friends with a dog has enriched your life.
Ruffian, my Newf companion, not only brings me laughter and comfort, and unconditional love, but she has rescued me from my despair after the sudden death of my husband of forty years. Together, we are navigating a new life filled with so many adventures.

Do you have any other pets; if so, what are their breeds and names?
I currently have four old Maine Coons, cats from the breeding program my husband Greg and I ran for many years. They are Harraseeket, Saratoga, Johnny Appleseed, and Chesuncook.

If you are a writer (either by trade or compulsion) what first drew you to the craft? If you're not a writer, why did you choose to write a piece for this anthology?
I have worked as an arts journalist for more than thirty years but came to fiction as a path through my grief. In paying tribute to a wealth of memories, I have forged another creative voice for myself – one that complements my arts writing and is very satisfying to me.

CAROL HANSON

CAROL HANSON

Where are you from?
Rochester Hills, Michigan.

Describe in one or two sentences how being friends with a dog has enriched your life.
As a child, we always had at least one dog. As an adult, I have had three miniature Schnauzers. I am a total dog person, and always loved their company and devotion. I couldn't imagine my life without one.

Do you have any other pets; if so, what are their breeds and names?
I have a miniature Schnauzer named Schatzi and a school of fish. All of their names start with the letter "S."

If you are a writer (either by trade or compulsion) what first drew you to the craft? If you're not a writer, why did you choose to write a piece for this anthology?
I love the creativity that comes from writing. I decided to write this story based on actual events.

CELIA P. RANSOM

CELIA P. RANSOM

Where are you from?
I have always lived in Michigan, currently in a suburb of Detroit. In summer you will find me and my husband in Northern Michigan.

Describe in one or two sentences how being friends with a dog has enriched your life.
Our Welsh Corgi adored us and we, her. She had such a sparkling personality. She was a constant and comforting companion. She was a god listener. We still miss her.

Do you have any other pets; if so, what are their breeds and names?
No.

If you are a writer (either by trade or compulsion) what first drew you to the craft? If you're not a writer, why did you choose to write a piece for this anthology?
I cannot remember when I haven't written. I began as a child by writing letters. This was before the time of technology and abbreviated thought and was a favored way of communication.

Celia's collection of poetry, *Poetry Plain & Simple,* was published by Grey Wolfe Publishing in 2014.

CHERYL GILLESPIE

Where are you from?
I now live in Falmouth, Maine, but I grew up in Winslow, Maine.

Describe in one or two sentences how being friends with a dog has enriched your life.
Dogs have always been an important part of my life and an incredible comfort to me in times of stress. As a toddler, I rode around on a St. Bernard called "Goofy," and I have cherished every dog in my life since then.

Do you have any other pets; if so, what are their breeds and names?
I'm afraid the only dogs in my life right now are the dear neighbors' dogs, such as the subject of this essay Powder and a charming old, chocolate Lab across the street who goes by the name of Bailey.

If you are a writer (either by trade or compulsion) what first drew you to the craft? If you're not a writer, why did you choose to write a piece for this anthology?
As a retired English teacher, I am a wannabe published writer, so I am trying to build my writing profile. I love the idea of a dog anthology and wanted to be part of it.

DANNY P. BARBARE

DANNY P. BARBARE

Where are you from?
The Upstate of the Carolinas.

Describe in one or two sentences how being friends with a dog has enriched your life.
A Barrel full of joy and craziness.

Do you have any other pets; if so, what are their breeds and names?
Miley, part Labrador and hound.

If you are a writer (either by trade or compulsion) what first drew you to the craft? If you're not a writer, why did you choose to write a piece for this anthology?
First as a therapy. Now just joy.

DARRELL LAURANT

DARRELL LAURANT

Where are you from?
Lake George, New York.

Describe in one or two sentences how being friends with a dog has enriched your life.
Living with dogs has taught me a lot about canine intelligence, which I think is vastly underrated. Our shepherd, for example, has been given the job of keeping squirrels out of the bird feeder this winter. When he sees a squirrel at the feeder, he will find us, whine, and urge us in his own way to open the sliding glass door to the rear deck so he can perform his duty. That's pretty smart, I think.

Do you have any other pets; if so, what are their breeds and names?
My three dogs are a German shepherd named Luke and two maltepoo brothers named Skittles and Pepper.

If you are a writer (either by trade or compulsion) what first drew you to the craft? If you're not a writer, why did you choose to write a piece for this anthology?
I'm a writer by trade, having retired last fall after forty years in the newspaper business to freelance full time. "Learning From Dogs" was just something I knocked out one morning while drinking my coffee, and I thought your book—read by dog owners—would be the perfect place to share it.

DENNIS KLOTZ

DENNIS KLOTZ

Where are you from?
The mean streets of Dearborn Heights, Michigan.

Describe in one or two sentences how being friends with a dog has enriched your life.
Whatever mood I'm in, be it happy or sad, a dog I will always be there for me. Their loyalty and their love is something I'll always carry with me.

Do you have any other pets; if so, what are their breeds and names?
Just Pepper, my Miniature Dachshund, who inspired the story.

If you are a writer (either by trade or compulsion) what first drew you to the craft? If you're not a writer, why did you choose to write a piece for this anthology?
I've always been a voracious reader and the short story really inspired me to write. It's a challenging form that when done well, can pack quite a powerful punch.

EILEEN VAN HOOK

Where are you from?
I'm a "Jersey Girl", currently living in the mountains of northwestern New Jersey.

Describe in one or two sentences how being friends with a dog has enriched your life.
Loving and being loved by a dog has made me more sensitive to the responsibility we have to speak out for the voiceless among us.

Do you have any other pets; if so, what are their breeds and names?
I had only Jake, my beloved dog, who went to sleep on January 21st, 2015, leaving me with warm memories and a heavy heart.

If you are a writer (either by trade or compulsion) what first drew you to the craft? If you're not a writer, why did you choose to write a piece for this anthology?
Writing allows me to express my creativity in a simple and meaningful way. All I need is a pen, a scrap of paper and my imagination.

ELISABETH WARD

Where are you from?
I now live in Southern California, but grew up in the Midwest and lived in the east for forty years. My dogs and I miss the snow but do enjoy a nice long spring.

Describe in one or two sentences how being friends with a dog has enriched your life.
When our children fell in love with the puppy Mushroom, our whole family was adopted by dogs. Letting Mushroom into our lives expanded not only our family but our horizons. We might be able to see those horizons better than a dog can, but we can't smell what's just beyond. We're always in need of their sense and senses.

Do you have any other pets; if so, what are their breeds and names?
We have a Weimaraner and an English pointer, a cat, three Icelandic horses, a small herd of cashmere goats, and chickens. They all have names and most of them come when called. Most of the time. Our two grown children have six dogs between them. It's a madhouse.

If you are a writer (either by trade or compulsion) what first drew you to the craft? If you're not a writer, why did you choose to write a piece for this anthology?
I am a writer (www.elisabethward.com) and choose to write for this anthology because I admire the gift it brings to animal welfare. When animals benefit, so do people. The service dog is living proof of that.

GARY BECK

GARY BECK

Where are you from?
New York City.

Describe in one or two sentences how being friends with a dog has enriched your life.
I learned to appreciate the pure nature of a loving dog.

Do you have any other pets; if so, what are their breeds and names?
No

If you are a writer (either by trade or compulsion) what first drew you to the craft? If you're not a writer, why did you choose to write a piece for this anthology?
I'm a writer and reading great writers drew me to the craft.

Gary Beck has spent most of his adult life as a theater director, and as an art dealer when he couldn't make a living in theater. He has eleven published chapbooks and one other accepted for publication. His poetry collections include *Days of Destruction* (Skive Press), *Expectations* (Rogue Scholars Press). *Dawn in Cities, Assault on Nature, Songs of a Clerk, Civilized Ways* (Winter Goose Publishing). *Perceptions and Displays* will be published by Winter Goose Publishing. His novels include: *Extreme Change* (Cogwheel Press) *Acts of Defiance* (Artema Press). *Flawed Connections* has been accepted for publication (Black Rose Writing). His short story collection, *A Glimpse of Youth* (Sweatshoppe Publications). His original plays and translations of Moliere, Aristophanes and Sophocles have been produced Off-Broadway. His poetry, fiction, and essays have appeared in hundreds of literary magazines. He currently lives in New York City

HUGH ANDERSON

HUGH ANDERSON

Where are you from?
Nanaimo, British Columbia, a mid-sized city on Vancouver Island off the Southwest Coast of Canada.

Describe in one or two sentences how being friends with a dog has enriched your life.
A dog's love is uncomplicated, but my dog's greatest gift is that she is a bridge between the human and the natural world. My walks with her open my eyes to things that I might not otherwise see.

Do you have any other pets; if so, what are their breeds and names?
No.

If you are a writer (either by trade or compulsion) what first drew you to the craft? If you're not a writer, why did you choose to write a piece for this anthology?
The world presents itself in image and story. As long as I can remember, because I have always been drawn to the music of language, the images have formed as words that ask to be shaped into poetry.

JOHN C. MANNONE

JOHN C. MANNONE

Where are you from?

I live in near Knoxville, Tennessee, grew up in Baltimore, Maryland, and, as a first generation Italian-born outside of Sicily, I was born in Montevideo, Uruguay as a U.S. citizen.

Describe in one or two sentences how being friends with a dog has enriched your life.

Perhaps my poetry says it best. My dog taught me a lot about what it meant to be human. Some of my greatest joys came from my dogs; some of my deepest sorrows overcame me when I lost them.

Do you have any other pets; if so, what are their breeds and names?

Not at the moment; just a stray cat who's taken up residence in my yard whom I have befriended.

If you are a writer (either by trade or compulsion) what first drew you to the craft? If you're not a writer, why did you choose to write a piece for this anthology?

I think it was F. Scott Fitzgerald that said it best (personalized and paraphrased): I don't write poetry because I have something to say, but I write poetry because something needs to be said. I am delighted that this anthology will remind us how loving our dogs are. I want to be part of that.

John C. Mannone has over 400 works accepted in literary venues such as The Southern Poetry Anthology (Volume VII, NC), Still: The Journal, Pine Mountain Sand & Gravel, Negative Capability, Split Rock Review, Tupelo Press, and The Baltimore Review. His collection, Flux Lines, was a semi-finalist for the 2014 Mary Ballard Poetry Chapbook Prize. He's the poetry editor for Silver Blade and Abyss & Apex, and an adjunct professor of chemistry and physics at Hiwassee College, Madisonville, TN. His work has been nominated three times for the Pushcart. And he loves big dogs. Visit The Art of Poetry: http://jcmannone.wordpress.com

KAGE ALAN

KAGE ALAN

Where are you from?
I grew up in the Fraser, Michigan area and have remained in the state all my life.

Describe in one or two sentences how being friends with a dog has enriched your life.
I was an only child, so my only consistent companion was my dog. When the two of you open your hearts to each other, there's no room for loneliness.

Do you have any other pets; if so, what are their breeds and names?
I have a hundred or so shrimp and some Neon Tetras in a tank... all of who I have named "fish" or "shrimp."

If you are a writer (either by trade or compulsion) what first drew you to the craft? If you're not a writer, why did you choose to write a piece for this anthology?
I've been writing stories since the first grade. I used to watch (and still do) films and TV shows where I felt the story should have continued. Why not develop a craft that allows one to do just that?

Kage Alan lives in a suburb of Detroit, MI with his husband and their fish and shrimp, who are affectionately named and answer to "fish" or "shrimp"...except his husband. He lives in fear of his husband's Hong Kong Grandmonster and is the author of several comedic novels and short stories within the GLBT genre.

MADELYN D. KAMEN

MADELYN D. KAMEN

Where are you from?
Houston, Texas.

Describe in one or two sentences how being friends with a dog has enriched your life.
I have no grandchildren, but I have six dogs. They love me, play with me, tease me, and destroy rugs, furniture, etc. They also eat pens and pencils. They have not yet learned to use the computer. Thank heavens.

Do you have any other pets; if so, what are their breeds and names?
Six is enough. They are all shih tzus and are the mother, father and four pup litter from the same family: Molly, Joey, Peanut, Pollywolly Sinatra, T-Rex, and Spot.

If you are a writer (either by trade or compulsion) what first drew you to the craft? If you're not a writer, why did you choose to write a piece for this anthology?
I write and love dogs.

MARY ANN BACK

MARY ANN BACK

Where are you from?
Mason, Ohio.

Describe in one or two sentences how being friends with a dog has enriched your life.
My dog, Max, the star of my story, "Hiding Fromm the Demon", is the love of my life. He follows me like a puppy and he's almost 11 years old. He sleeps with me, cuddles with me, lays at my feet, plays with me, and makes me laugh. On Sunday mornings, when I get up and read the paper, I'm not paying attention to him so he jumps into my lap (all 40 pounds of him) and crashes through the newspaper! Sadly he is very afraid of thunderstorms.

Do you have any other pets; if so, what are their breeds and names?
No other pets right now. I used to have a parakeet that followed me all over the house. I loved that bird!

If you are a writer (either by trade or compulsion) what first drew you to the craft? If you're not a writer, why did you choose to write a piece for this anthology?
I've been writing on and off since grade school. My teacher asked us to write short stories and he loved mine. It just seemed to come naturally. I love it!

MATT MCGEE

Where are you from?

Bi-coastal. Have lived in Thousand Oaks, California for 35 years but a part of me still and always will belong to Vestal, New York.

Describe in one or two sentences how being friends with a dog has enriched your life.

You know how when you're in high school you float through the halls picking out the friendly faces, kind of like jumping from rock to rock until you're safely across the stream? My daily life, as it's lived outside my home for 14-20 hours a day, is a bit like this – and the friendliest faces are always the dogs I encounter. I get along with humans just as well, but the boundless appreciation a dog shows a friendly human in unparalleled.

Do you have any other pets; if so, what are their breeds and names?

Her name is Theobald and she's a white domesticated rabbit with dark circles around her eyes that looks like Courtney Love-esque heavy eyeliner. She's allowed free reign of our backyard as it's fenced and there are no predators. She eats all the vegetable scraps the house can produce plus alfalfa and a little of everything that grows in the yard

If you are a writer (either by trade or compulsion) what first drew you to the craft? If you're not a writer, why did you choose to write a piece for this anthology?

George Burns lived to be 100. Everyone who interviewed him asked 'what's the secret to living a long life, what's the secret to a long life?' He'd make some joke about it then say 'you have to get up every day and have something to do - otherwise you never want to get out of bed.' I started with an innate aptitude for spelling and grammar around age six. Now reading, writing and spelling make me want to get up every day.

MICHAELEEN KELLY

MICHAELEEN KELLY

Where are you from?
Grand Rapids, Michigan.

Describe in one or two sentences how being friends with a dog has enriched your life.
I have drawn enormous support and comfort through difficult times from my dogs. Their presence in my home has provided me with innumerable opportunities for imaginative conversations and narratives regarding our shared lives.

Do you have any other pets; if so, what are their breeds and names?
No.

If you are a writer (either by trade or compulsion) what first drew you to the craft? If you're not a writer, why did you choose to write a piece for this anthology?
I have primarily written philosophical articles as a philosophy professor, but with the death of my son, I was drawn to poetry as a resource for enlightenment and joy.

NANCY J. SHATTUCK

NANCY J. SHATTUCK

Where are you from?
I was born in Ypsilanti, Michigan, and lived in the Detroit area for all but the thirty years that I lived in St. Louis, Missouri. At least some of my time in Michigan was spent on farms, where I learned to love animals. We had quite a menagerie: dogs, cats, horses, cows, pigs, chickens, and ducks.

Describe in one or two sentences how being friends with a dog has enriched your life.
My first experience with a pet was a Collie puppy, Tippy Tippy Tay, who was tragically killed in a car accident. That formative experience at age five led me to a life of pampering animals. I have never been without a pet since then, even when it was smuggling a kitten into my bed at night.

Do you have any other pets; if so, what are their breeds and names?
My cats Lynx and Buttons, both street rescues, are now about eighteen years old and will break my heart when they go, but I'll have many friends waiting at the animal shelters for a home.

If you are a writer (either by trade or compulsion) what first drew you to the craft? If you're not a writer, why did you choose to write a piece for this anthology?
I can honestly say I have been writing since I was three; not knowing my letters did not stop me from scribbling for hours! At first, I was merely emulating the young adults in our family, showing them I could write, too, but my love of stories followed soon after. Everyone read aloud to me. By the time I started school, I was a big copycat; I wanted to be just like the writers and story tellers! I never stopped writing.

NEIL DOHERTY

NEIL DOHERTY

Where are you from?
Living in Bainbridge Island but originally from Liverpool, England

Describe in one or two sentences how being friends with a dog has enriched your life.
They listen with intense concentration when I read my poetry to them.

NICOLE KOPPIN

NICOLE KOPPIN

Where are you from?
Madison Heights, Michigan.

Describe in one or two sentences how being friends with a dog has enriched your life.
Both of my dogs bring so much joy into my life, from the goofy looks they give to the happy dance they do when I get home from work. No matter how rough my day has been when I come home my pups know exactly how to make it all better!

Do you have any other pets; if so, what are their breeds and names?
I have two dogs, Vixen a German Spitz mix and Mack a Beagle Pit Bull mix. I also have two cats, Lynx is a domestic shorthair and Phira is a domestic long-hair.

If you are a writer (either by trade or compulsion) what first drew you to the craft? If you're not a writer, why did you choose to write a piece for this anthology?
I am not a professional writer, but I have always enjoyed writing as a release. I wanted to write a piece for this anthology because I think it is a wonderful cause and would love to be a part of it!

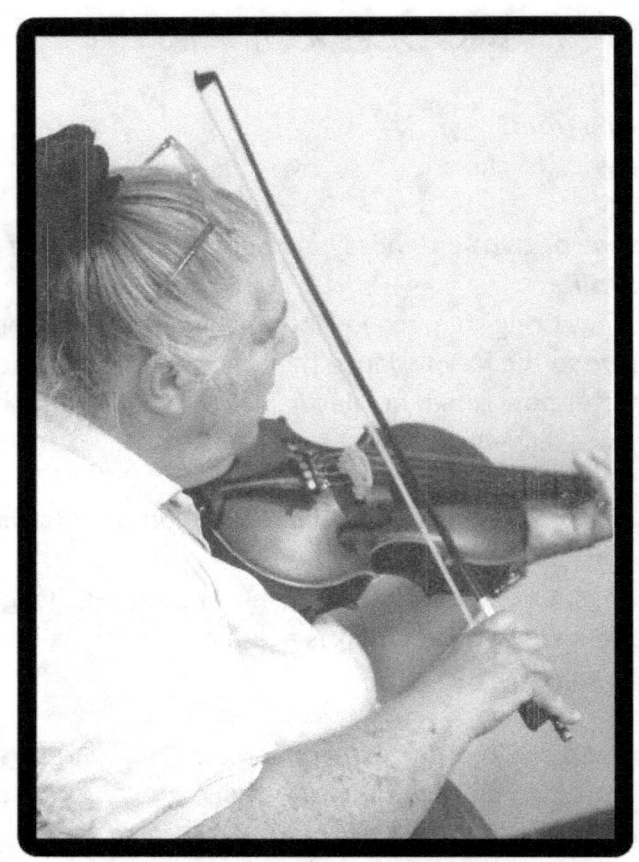

PATRICIA HOLLAND

PATRICIA HOLLAND

Where are you from?

Paris, Kentucky. There are more horses than people in my county. I love watching the Thoroughbred foals racing around their pasture as if it's the Kentucky Derby. In just three years, one of them may win that race!

Describe in one or two sentences how being friends with a dog has enriched your life.

Over my lifetime, I've adopted several dogs from our local animal shelter. Cloud, the inspiration for my story, was underweight at 66 pounds when I adopted him. The folks at the shelter told me he was probably a yellow Lab under a year old "...so he might grow a bit more." Over the next year, he turned white and kept growing. When he hit 170 pounds a friend, who judges AKC dog shows took one look and said, "That's the biggest Great Pyrenees I've ever seen. He's as big as a couch."

Do you have any other pets; if so, what are their breeds and names?

I take in abused horses. After they arrive on my farm, they have a life lease on the place.

If you are a writer (either by trade or compulsion) what first drew you to the craft? If you're not a writer, why did you choose to write a piece for this anthology?

I admire the Grey Wolfe Publishing team and their goal to bring awareness to the roles dogs play in our lives. My dog Cloud fiercely guards the livestock from coyotes but is very gentle with my family.

PHILIPPE SHILS

PHILIPPE SHILS

Where are you from?
Decatur, Illinois.

Describe in one or two sentences how being friends with a dog has enriched your life.
My dogs are more than friend—they're family. We quarrel but always with the knowledge that our relationship is secure.

Do you have any other pets; if so, what are their breeds and names?
Some cats, some fish, some dogs.

If you are a writer (either by trade or compulsion) what first drew you to the craft? If you're not a writer, why did you choose to write a piece for this anthology?
What else to do with the thoughts that tumble around my brain but organize them somehow?

RICK BLUM

RICK BLUM

Where are you from?
I currently live in Chelmsford, Massachusetts. However, by the time this anthology is published, I will have moved to Bedford, Massachusetts.

Describe in one or two sentences how being friends with a dog has enriched your life.
I don't know if dogs are man's best friend, but they have been darn good companions for me since childhood when Sputnik and I romped throughout the neighborhood. Though my romping is now mostly confined to games of fetch, my pet dog is still a reliable source of fun and peacefulness.

Do you have any other pets; if so, what are their breeds and names?
Currently, a six-month-old dorky (Dachshund-Yorkshire terrier mix) named Lulu lives with my wife and me. (The cockapoo about whom these poems were written died last fall.)

If you are a writer (either by trade or compulsion) what first drew you to the craft? If you're not a writer, why did you choose to write a piece for this anthology?
My first creative writings were op-ed-style essays chronicling humorous situations I experienced in business and everyday life – which provided a relief valve for pent-up frustrations that otherwise my wife would have had to endure alone. I later turned to poetry as a new creative venue for expression as well as a writing challenge.

S. JAGATHSIMHAN NAIR

Where are you from?
Thiruvananthapuram, India.

Describe in one or two sentences how being friends with a dog has enriched your life.
I thought about the dog I had a few years back. I remember how terribly sad, forlorn and upset it was during the three days my five-year-old son left us to spend his school holidays with my brother who lived some distance away.

Do you have any other pets; if so, what are their breeds and names?
No.

If you are a writer (either by trade or compulsion) what first drew you to the craft? If you're not a writer, why did you choose to write a piece for this anthology?
An American friend of mine gave me your address asking me to write. I thought it worth a try.

SARAH FRANCES MORAN

SARAH FRANCES MORAN

Where are you from?
Waco, Texas.

Describe in one or two sentences how being friends with a dog has enriched your life.
Nina, my Chihuahua, is my best friend. Every dog I've ever had has been my best friend. It is indescribable the way their company has enriched my life. Nina especially feels like a mini extension of my soul.

Do you have any other pets; if so, what are their breeds and names?
I have three other dogs: Sookie (Chihuahua-Rat Terrier Mix), Che (Chihuahua) and Bear (Toy Poodle). I also have two domestic shorthair cats: Sheba and Indi.

If you are a writer (either by trade or compulsion) what first drew you to the craft? If you're not a writer, why did you choose to write a piece for this anthology?
I began writing as a way to help others cope. My first poem was for a friend who was having a rough time. I write now about the things I'm passionate about or the things I feel need awareness in the world.

SARAH Z. SLEEPER

SARAH Z. SLEEPER

Where are you from?
Solana Beach, California.

Describe in one or two sentences how being friends with a dog has enriched your life.
I am the proud mom to two beautiful adopted mutts, Max, and Mini, who make every day sweeter, richer and more fun. As well, I'm a dedicated animal shelter volunteer.

Do you have any other pets; if so, what are their breeds and names?
Dixie, cat, rescued from under a building in Northern Michigan.

If you are a writer (either by trade or compulsion) what first drew you to the craft? If you're not a writer, why did you choose to write a piece for this anthology?
Ever since I read *Wind in the Willows* in grade school, I wanted to be a writer. Luckily, I am able to make a living at it. I chose to submit to *Write to Woof* because I believe that all dogs, service, shelter or otherwise, deserve a beautiful life. My poem was inspired by the many strays I saw as I traveled through Ecuador. Despite the splendor of the country, the plight of the dogs broke my heart.

SHANNON WAITE

SHANNON WAITE

Where are you from?
I grew up in Warren, Michigan where I currently still live.

Describe in one or two sentences how being friends with a dog has enriched your life.
My family had owned dogs all of my life growing up, and having a companion who was always willing to have fun was very encouraging.

Do you have any other pets; if so, what are their breeds and names?
Among being a dog lover, I also love raising hamsters; at the moment, I have one adorable little hamster named James.

If you are a writer (either by trade or compulsion) what first drew you to the craft? If you're not a writer, why did you choose to write a piece for this anthology?
Since I can remember, I was always a writer and illustrator; all I wanted to do was go back to the room to write and draw when my family went to Disney World. I think that I enjoy creating, and with writing, I love the art and expression that word choice provides.

http://www.shannonwaiteauthor.weebly.com

SHAY CAROLINE SIMMONS

Where are you from?
Ferndale, Michigan.

Describe in one or two sentences how being friends with a dog has enriched your life.
Dogs have completely changed my life for the better.

Do you have any other pets; if so, what are their breeds and names?
Skittles, Aussie Shepherd mix.

If you are a writer (either by trade or compulsion) what first drew you to the craft? If you're not a writer, why did you choose to write a piece for this anthology?
It's what I am passionate about.

STACY FRITZ

STACY FRITZ

Where are you from?
I currently reside in Lexington, Michigan. A lovely little place situated on Lake Huron in the Thumb area. I am originally from Whitmore Lake, MI.

Describe in one or two sentences how being friends with a dog has enriched your life.
As a kid, my dog was my buddy and playmate. As an adult, my dogs are still my buddies (and furry kids) who make me smile and laugh, remind me to enjoy the little things, to no sweat the things that don't matter and make me feel loved.

Do you have any other pets; if so, what are their breeds and names?
Currently, I also have a big white rabbit named Paws, a Lovebird named Kiwi, four rats (the girls, Licorice and Truffle, and the boys, Nutmeg and Fluffernutter), and fish (Larry, Moe, Curly, Shemp).

If you are a writer (either by trade or compulsion) what first drew you to the craft? If you're not a writer, why did you choose to write a piece for this anthology?
Growing up, I loved regaling my peers with stories, often scaring them into a sleepless night. I realized that stories that are told well can bring about a strong emotional reaction. In writing, I realized I could touch lives, at least for a moment. Now, I teach writing courses in high school, further touching lives through writing.

LEADER DOGS FOR THE BLIND
ROCHESTER, MICHIGAN

LEADER DOGS FOR THE BLIND
ROCHESTER, MICHIGAN

Our mission is empowering people who are blind, visually impaired or Deaf-Blind with lifelong skills for independent travel through quality Leader Dogs, highly effective client instruction and innovative services.

In support of this mission, our actions are guided, supported and measured by our values:

Respect and compassion for people and dogs
Passion for the work
Safety in all we do
Doing what is right
Innovation in our field
Teamwork
Superior experience for our stakeholders

Leader Dogs for the Blind
1039 S. Rochester Rd.
Rochester Hills, MI 48307-3115
248-651-9011
888-777-5332
TTY: 248-651-3713
www.leaderdog.org